The
WORMWOOD
E-MAILS

Adele H. Lewis

ISBN 978-1-64471-006-7 (Paperback)
ISBN 978-1-64471-007-4 (Digital)

Covenant Books, Inc.
11661 Hwy 707
Murrells Inlet, SC 29576
www.covenantbooks.com

Thus, if I laugh at you, O fellow-men! If I trace with curious interest your labyrinthine self-delusions, note the inconsistencies in your zealous adhesions, and smile at your helpless endeavors in a rashly chosen part, it is not that I feel myself aloof from you: the more intimately I seem to discern your weaknesses, the stronger to me is the proof that I share them. How otherwise could I get the discernment? For even what we are averse to, what we vow not to entertain, must have shaped or shadowed itself within us as a possibility before we can think of exorcising it. No man can know his brother simply as a spectator. Dear blunderers, I am one of you.

—George Eliot, *The Impressions of Theophrastus Such*

CONTENTS

Spin a Sticky Web

My Dear Tempters,

We do indeed wage, "by force or guile, eternal war."[*] The work of tempting is expansive, exacting, and yields its fruits to the trained and experienced demon. I fondly remember advice given to me early in my career by veteran tempters and, thus, decided likewise to pass on words of counsel and caution to this younger generation in their initial assignments. Times having changed considerably (notice I am sending a group e-mail rather than posting letters), I expect to update the avenues of effort and effectiveness that these more modern times require. I hope in saying this, none of you will assume that *all* things have changed and you can disregard the past work of our inexorable Father.

Most aspects of human nature never change; so while these e-mails might discuss new methods, the aims, possibilities, and trajectories of temptations will be consistent, as is the Enemy's still-dangerous desire and motivations for his "children." Indeed, these days we have to work overtime as you will soon see. Since my younger days as a Junior Tempter, a veritable deluge of disgusting light has been flooding throughout the entire world. If we are not careful *and* consistent, humans might perceive a few things in this new light. We here at headquarters are quite concerned, despite the great advances we made in turning humans away from truth in the last century. We take pride in the fact that we are "on the spot" whenever anything of import happens in the Enemy's camp. Very often, we can turn things to our advantage, and though there have been some failures, for the

---

[*] John Milton, *Paradise Lost*, (London, 2014), I.21.

7

most part, we are quick to take the offensive. Thus, you will need to be up-to-date in your methods and grasp the potential advantages inherent in this modern era.

There is no time to be lost as the Enemy's forces are out in full. They are organized. They are steadfast in their loyalty to him, and what is worse—*they have his help!* He is despicable that way. Make sure you take notes on the pointers I will be giving and then practice until you are adept at what you do. We need trenchant observations followed by quick cunning action. No weak dilettantes will do. You will learn to entwine your patients with almost imperceptible cords, which ultimately form a bond so constricting they cannot escape. By the time they perceive the tightening, it will be too late.

The trick is to learn to fetter with a light hand. There is a subtlety and art in the work that you have yet to master, hence these e-mails! Don't concern yourself with anonymity. These times call for bold and bellicose plans. It matters little whether or not humans are aware of our existence. They can either be induced to paranoia to the point of blaming all the ills of life on us and, therefore, take little responsibility themselves, or they can be lulled into complacency by denying our very existence. Thankfully, the contemporary world chooses the latter.

The most important initial concept to grasp is the interrelatedness of various temptations. It is like the sticky web of a spider. One long thin strand may catch someone; however, it is usually not enough. They can too easily extricate themselves, and they will have the help of others to do it. That is why all the strands of a web are connected. Humans will blunder into one mistake, and it will soon lead to another until, eventually, they will be firmly caught.

Vices, as well as the more seemingly innocuous habits, should always develop into another one. Keep a long list in your head so you will be ready to spin out the various interrelated traps. For example, keeping a human from Sabbath devotional services for any length of time will soon lead to a feeling of estrangement from his fellow churchgoers. He will then imagine—with your help—all sorts of judgment coming from them. This will, hopefully, create animosity that extends in multiple directions and into various spheres. He is then even less inclined to be part of their fellowship. Do you see the beauty of it? Thoughts lead to actions, and actions lead to habits, which—over time—will lead to a fixed and resolute character. The only problem with this axiom is that it can work in the Enemy's direction as well.

Best,
Wormwood

PS In case you are wondering about my qualifications to be giving advice, I am presently a Senior Officer of Enticement on the university's board of regents. I myself have worked my way to this position largely by force and guile.

There Is an App for Everything!

My Dear Tempters,

O ne of the first bits of advice I can give you is to use technology to your advantage. The Enemy certainly has and will continue to do so. It is your job to keep your patient's connection to the online world just that—connected to *the world*—for it can, of course, bring him closer to the Enemy in ways not even dreamed of fifty years ago. With just a few clicks, they can have access to sermons, songs, fellow believer's testimonies, and even those odious books of scripture that can strengthen them so. They can see beautiful images and read heart-warming stories. They can communicate with fellow believers and receive help and direction from the worst of them, all within minutes and at any hour of the day or night. The publication of books and pamphlets and their purchase used to be tedious and expensive. Even earlier, there were happy days when there were no printed materials and only the hierarchy of the church had access to what is among them (most disturbingly) called the "Word of God." All that is past, and we must be on the offensive to keep this propaganda out of their reach. For now there are individual believer's blogs, seminar and institute reports and papers, and beautifully illustrated scripture quotations floating through cyberspace and church Facebook pages. There are even (though it is hard to credit) devoted intellectuals that are influencing people with well-worded and faith-filled apologetics.

In just a few seconds, humans can find enough material to undo years of our most diligent efforts. Of course, on the other side, our *best* material—both from ages past and more current atheistic and pejorative trends—is also available at the touch of a mouse click. Therefore, if your patient is going to be searching, you can direct him to *that* material—which is most abundant. Often in the pursuit of good, the search engines of the Internet (which we, for the most part, control) will take them into *our* camp and there you can try to grab them with disturbing innuendos and half-truths (even salacious imagery) before they even realize what has happened.

However, if you cannot influence your patient with *our* material, you can most effectively keep *their* material out of reach by having technology become a distraction that distances them from spiritual matters. Here some of the best of our Father's followers have provided the creativity and technical savvy to flood the world with an almost endless array of apps and websites, games and movies. Humans little realize that the talent for such kinds of creation can work for our side just as much as for the Enemy's.

Just the other day, I saw a whole group of young girls taking some kind of online test on their phones to see what famous actress they were—ahhh! Just the sort of inane waste of time we like to cultivate. There are endless examples of this currently thriving, and more is coming. We can get humans to sit in front of a computer screen for *hours* and think nothing of the passing of time. Computers, laptops, tablets, iPads, iPhones—anything with a screen! Even if they begin with some important subject, we can pull a great many other things into their line of vision—thus moving them on to yet another distraction. Let us say your patient was reading something beneficial and stopped, pulled out his phone, and went to Dictionary.com to look up a word with which he was unfamiliar. So far, quite harmless, but we have managed to put lots of other things on the screen to keep him from going back to his book. He will have some curiosity about a news headline, perhaps, and click over to that (maybe moving on to several news items). Then we can get the bikini-clad model advertising something to catch his attention, and *poof*—the book is forgotten. Distraction! Distraction! Use technology as a distraction from *whom* and *what* is most important. Not only does it distract them from communicating with each other, but also it will eventually help to dull the mind and spirit to such a point that the Enemy hasn't much chance of communication with the poor souls. Moreover, it only requires the smallest of screens. The screen is one of our most hallowed inventions; beginning with the TV in the 1950s and on to the present, you will notice there are now screens everywhere: the gas station pump, the grocery checkout line—the poor vermin cannot get away from them!

If you need further proof of technology's effectiveness, go into any church meeting, and you can see many individuals—not just teenagers, mind you—looking at their little screens rather than at their sacrament table or the pulpit. Technology can keep them from the immediate and important, even when they are physically *within* a church building attending services. Humans believe their minds can concentrate on more than one thing at a time. We know better. Gradually, without even realizing it, they can go through their day, downloading this and streaming that, moving inexorably to a life of pure technology. They have not had had one tender, meaningful, *real* moment with their fellow humans, their own souls, and certainly not with the Enemy.

Of course, technology is a great avenue for spending more money. Continually encourage that. There is always something new to buy. Create the idea in their minds that if they do not have the latest technology in their hands immediately, they will be out of date and out of step among their friends and within society. Technology is our Zeitgeist, and we must be assiduous in our work of total immersion and complete addiction—technology obsession, technology possession, technology debt, technology language, technology invention; in other words, total allegiance to the god of technology.

Best,
Wormwood

THE BATTLE OF SELF

My Dear Tempters,

One of your highest priorities, if not *the* most important one, is your attention to what we call "the Battle of Self." Humans, in their natural state, are most often focused upon themselves—what they are feeling, what they want, how they are being treated, what they imagine themselves to need, how circumstances affect them— that is the usual condition. In fact, the Enemy based his admonition of loving their neighbor as themselves on this premise. For, if they had the same kind of concern and interest in others that they do for themselves, there would be peace and harmony and help for all.*

Our efforts are targeted at keeping this natural focus on them- selves rather than allowing it turn to others. For when they do that, they forget about themselves, and we have lost the battle. Most humans, though, have to try and manually (if you will) think of others. They mistakenly believe if they try hard enough they will be able to. What the Enemy wants is for them to focus on him and that will eventually influence them to focus on others. If they are at all (or have been) in the Enemy's camp, they will feel him working on this natural self-centered state and try to help them forget "Self" and direct their attention to him. This will usually cause a delightful conflict inside them as their natural-self state will war against what they are being prodded (by the Enemy) to do and to be. What we want is to have them firmly focused on themselves. Keep the battle raging. Even their focus on the battle itself (if they are smart enough to apprehend it) will keep them centered on themselves.

There is a strange paradox promoted by the Enemy's camp that only in losing oneself, can one actually find oneself. In other words, he has designed humans in such a way that only in giving up what they are naturally inclined to keep—their own self welfare, or preservation, or whatever you want to call it—will they, in the end actually have a *real* "Self." Fortunately, most of them are too dull-minded to grasp this seemingly contradictory concept, but you will sometimes encounter one that has had a brief glimpse of light from time to time, and so will be harder to fool. You may encounter one or two of your patients having a moment of self-revelation and then they clearly perceive our militant strategy. As one of their writers musingly asked, "*...was there no escape here from this stupidity of a murmuring self-occupation?*" Humans also have some faint inclinations to look around, to forget themselves, and even in extreme cases to give their life for someone else—those impulses can be strengthened by the Enemy. Avoid this at all costs! That is why it is a war. Keep the "Self" winning battles day after day, and the opposite impulse will soon fade away almost completely.

One very clever ruse we have established is the belief that in focusing on themselves *first* they will better be able to help others. Now in theory this might perhaps be true. An example of this principle is when the flight attendant on an airplane tells people traveling with children to secure their own air mask *first* before helping their children. Logically, this makes sense as you would have a hard time helping your child if you were about to pass out! This policy can extend to other areas of life. You cannot give to others if you do not have anything to give. The key here is the word *first*. We can easily turn the principle into a refusal to help someone in need with the excuse that one must save one's strength or build it up first, *then*, one will readily help. Many humans have been led to concentrate wholly on themselves with this argument. They never do seem to get to the point of being able to give their means, or time or attention to others, because they do not move beyond the "building up" of their own strength phase.

There was a campaign we started some years ago that is particularly effective with women who usually have too much to do. It went

---

* Eliot, *Theophrastus Such*, (New York, 1879), 15.

like this: "Learn to say no! You cannot do everything you want to, so you have to pace yourself and be willing to say no so you are not so overwhelmed that you cannot do any good." So once again, a true principle was distorted into encouraging many people to say no to things they really *could* have said yes to: calls for help, friends in need, service projects, menial tasks.

Here again, we have the help of the world of business at our disposal—as we should—since we have spent many hours winning them to our side. Society today markets "Self" products by the millions, from clothes to cars to finance books. Thousands of our followers try endlessly to keep the "Self" satisfied (which also keeps the "Self" distracted from important things). Remember the old jingle of McDonald's from years ago, (which incidentally, we inspired), *"You deserve a break today, so get out and get away..."* You see what I mean? Even though it was just to sell hamburgers, it was exactly the philosophy we wanted to instill. You *deserve* something, anything, and usually a lot more than you presently have, whether it is lunch, or time, or money, or attention, or opportunities. You will see how this fits in with our plans in the health and body area—more of that in another e-mail.

Every day there is some new advertisement, which takes advantage of human feebleness with slick sales gimmicks. Even seemingly innocuous or beneficial products can help. The pharmaceutical companies have made tremendous strides in conditioning humans to believe that every ailment, no matter how slight, should have a remedy if they are willing to pay for it. Their advertisements appeal to the notion of taking care of number one, so you can live a real, full life. (By the way, I hope you are watching the TV so you comprehend our methodology.) Little do they realize the Enemy wants them to take care of the rest of the numbers, no matter what the state of their health is, for that is how they actually *can* live a full, *real* life. Keep anything resembling this thought out of their minds.

There are additional avenues of temptation we can offer in this area of "Self." It is not just in the helping of others that we can work—as "Self" looms large in any interaction between humans. All sorts of problems can be cultivated in their relationships by the focus on "Self." As they concentrate on how they are "*made to feel*" by others, we can easily introduce offense, isolation, misunderstanding, inadequacies, ego and certainly enmity between them. You see the genius in the words "*made to feel*." Humans are foolish enough to think that how they feel is something beyond them, that they do not "choose" to feel a certain way but are impelled to by forces (and people) outside their control. We capitalize on that error and at the same time concentrate our efforts on the "Self," thereby causing some wonderful problems between them. Both ends of the spectrum are available to us. Either create hypersensitivity in your patient that sees every conversation as stultifying, making him feel worse *about himself* and, thereby, worse about them—or foster the condition of him coming away from every interaction with others feeling that *he* is a pretty good man for whatever *he* has said or done, and the attendant feeling of not being appreciated nearly enough.

You see, do you not, how the focus is on "Self" and not the person he has interacted with? Have the conversation always be about him. Prevent any real interest in the welfare of those he is talking with enter his mind and certainly not his heart! The sine qua non of our work is to prevent the Enemy from getting his foot in the door, so avoidance of the heart is essential. One fact so obvious to us but apparently not to modern society is that if humans would forget about themselves, they would all get along much better. It is the prideful *me* that screams out in all those contentious blogs and Facebook posts. The *me* approach usually generates lengthy and acrimonious online "discussions" that only serve to reinforce everyone's original belief, rather than bringing real understanding. Humans cannot understand one another while they are concentrating on themselves. The feelings of being shunned, misunderstood, and discriminated against—even if they are from legitimate experiences—would not be nearly so significant if the focus was on others rather than on "Self." Focusing on others allows humans to go through difficulties and not only bear them but become better because of them. Thankfully, this is the exception rather than the rule with adversity.

Of course there is also another tact that you can take with those who actually *do* spend much of their time serving others. Remind them how sacrificial they *are* being and foster the "martyr" attitude. And of course, they need to advertise what they are doing—none of the "not letting their right hand know what their left hand is doing" business. This will cause them to turn their thoughts back to themselves, with a well-deserved pat on the back. You can also take the tack of suggesting just how *very* much of their time is spent on others, most of whom do not appreciate it. Either way, they will turn from those they serve, to themselves, in both their thoughts and heart—that is the key.

Another tendency to cultivate is the human desire for attention, approval and admiration. They cannot quite help themselves. Apparently, humans are so unsteady in their own estimation (see the next e-mail), they are constantly seeking some kind of self-affirmation in the form of laudatory praise, or if that fails, just mere attention—even negative will do. So, with our recent inroads in the form of social media, the opportunities for this kind of self-promotion are *endless* and *constant!* I trust I do not even have to proffer suggestions—you are well up to the task.

This society has been so well-trained at thinking in terms of rights and privileges and so little about responsibility, accountability and true charity, that our job is much easier than it has been in the past. We have been quite successful in squeezing out any real altruism among them. Even the celebrities with their grandiose "save the world" causes can manipulate the whole scheme to ensure a perfect photo op and free advertising for their next film (or football game). The attention stays focused wholly on them and not on those they are helping. How wonderfully the media is our ally here as in so many other ways! There is also the additional effect on the masses watching and listening to these famous "deeds." It generates not, "*I wish I could help others too*" feelings but "*I wish I was like them*" feelings. So rather than your patient helping his neighbor, he can create an imaginary desire to help the poor people in Darfur and neglect those closest to him—of course, there are the few obscure patients who really, actually do both; but thankfully, there are not many of them). So then with both the celebrity and the obscure admirer, the focus is clearly on "Self." That is your goal!

Best,
Wormwood

*I know you will argue there are those individuals who really do *not* like themselves and so this premise is a false one. However, even humans who fairly loathe themselves will exhibit self-preservation and preoccupation—so the admonition by the Enemy still stands.

"Selfie" Esteem

My Dear Tempters,

As a supplement to the last email on the Battle of Self, I want to make clear some important related points. What you need to understand is the Myth of Self-esteem. We have had such delight in this particular deception because it is something so central to the Enemy and his nature. Humans are his children and he loves them. In fact, he loves them so much he sent his son to die for them. That is *the* most basic of the tenants of the Christian faith. And yet, even with the words of John 3:16 ringing in their ears—please stop cringing; we have to know what the Enemy is saying, so I will sometimes refer specifically to the source—I say, even with the words ringing in their ears, they so often question their own worth. How the fatuous fools *can*—when they know this is beyond our comprehension—but they do. They can search their whole lives not only for meaning but also for reasons to think well of themselves. So what we have very cleverly instilled in them *is the search* for this abstract concept of Self-esteem. We have put it in their heads that if only they (fill in the blank here), then they will feel good about themselves—they will *have* Self-esteem. We then provide an endless supply of concepts to put in that blank. For example: one of our best is the perfect body. This is especially effective with women. They are under the mistaken impression that if they are some ideal size and weight, they will *have* Self-esteem.

We worked with a woman once who considered herself about fifty pounds overweight. Her notion of ideal weight did not come from her physician but rather from advertising and media. Her daughter attended a local high school and one day, while dropping her off she noticed a woman working in the office she had gone to high school with many years ago. Rather than speaking to her, she quickly got in her car and left—for her friend from high school still looked thin and fit and here she was, so much larger. She felt badly about herself, just where we wanted her! However, lest you think that our toil was at an end, hear the rest of the story. This woman worked hard at eating healthy and exercising and over a period of a few months lost the fifty pounds. The next time she went to the school after the weight loss, it occurred to her that she would not at all mind running into the old friend now, for she felt good about herself. Again, just where we want her! She had *acquired* Self-esteem because now she looked better! So you see, it does not matter if someone feels badly about themselves or good about themselves— what matters is keeping them in the delusion that their Self-esteem comes from a source other than who they really are, which is a child of the Enemy. Humans do not realize that any thought of themselves— which we try to maintain and the Enemy tries to repress—*any* thought one way or another, is artificial and ineffectual in his plan. Moreover, we have convinced them that without Self-esteem they cannot do anything. (See the last e-mail on the Battle of Self—we hope they do not stop trying to *find* themselves the silly people!)

The possibilities for the blank that precedes Self-esteem are as diverse as they are endless. They range from having expensive clothes and nice homes, to a PhD or prestigious governmental office or successful children. It really does not matter what is in the blank—as they rarely figure out it is the blank itself that is a lie. Humans *cannot* manufacture Self-esteem. They *cannot* acquire it. They *cannot* build it up or tear it down. They *cannot* find it by looking, or develop it by any method. *It does not exist!* Their worth is not in jeopardy or changeable or even in question. It is intrinsic to who they *are*, and you must be careful here for if they get anywhere near to *that* understanding, you will need to distance them from it as quickly and firmly as possible. Don't let them near the scriptural injunction about losing their life to find it—at all costs—for if they start pondering that concept they will get near to the truth of the matter. Nothing outside of the unalterable fact—that they really *are* the children of the Enemy and he really *did* send his son to earth for their sakes—

will create in them Self-esteem. The whole concept is a construct. We created it and we keep it flourishing. The contemporary world aids our cause with its emphasis on material culture. There is so much out there to buy, so many new fashions to try, and so many ways to adorn the body and the psyche, that humans can spend their whole life working on themselves and never question the value of what they are doing.

We have inextricably linked this notion to the delightful vice of comparison. Humans base their ideas of Self-esteem on how they measure up to an ideal, derived from comparison to others. For what really *is* financial success? It would be different in the middle of Cairo to what it is in Houston. How large is a large house? What are expensive clothes? How expensive? What is being smart enough or sophisticated enough? How many degrees? How big of a paycheck? These are all relative, and have no concrete reality. They only exist in the world of comparison. So as humans have the propensity to look around them and compare their plight with others, we can persuade them that if they had a certain job or haircut or profession, they would feel good about themselves.

One more recent success of ours in this department is the lengths to which women will go (we are working on the men, as we speak) on surgically altering their bodies to create the ideal. We used to push this just as an alternative for defying the aging process, but even we have been amazed at how many young women we have been able to talk into justifying expensive (and often risky) surgery to look as they think they should (based of course on the ideal which has been constructed in *comparison*). We are quite delighted as they make these choices by rationalizing that they *need* to feel good about themselves and this will do it!

Once again, how it is that they do not comprehend that they will never have this elusive Self-esteem by looking for it, working on it, paying for it—I don't know. For none of these things bring it—it is not real! Keep it quiet though…

Best,
Wormwood

Homage to Hollywood

My Dear Tempters,

I understand from one of your e-mails that a patient has just purchased a seventy-two-inch TV. This is good news indeed. Well done. You managed to persuade him that it was rather a necessity and that he would be behind the times if he continued with the smaller version. One of our greatest triumphs in this modern age has been in the area of entertainment. In generations past, we had some good vices, but even those who were indulgent generally acknowledged them as vices. Now, with the full flowering of what I just like to term, "Hollywood," we have entertainment brought to a whole new level with all the detriments and none of the moderation, embarrassment or shame of the sins of ages past. Whereas formerly, attending the Saturday matinee was a good release from a hard week of work and innocent entertainment, today we have the pursuit of entertainment as a full time endeavor. Great numbers are on our side and in our employ (most without realizing it), and humans spend millions of dollars in its creation and consumption. Entertainment is considered by many to be harmless and innocent, a nice diversion from real life. What they do not realize is that it has the power not just to reflect life but also to shape it.

Take that TV comedy show some years ago about six friends who lived together and went through all sorts of daily dilemmas. Due to the lightheartedness of the show and the inclination toward humor, we were able to develop and encourage in millions of youthful watchers a very casual and false idea about human intimacy. Young adults today can quote whole episodes from memory, some of which were quite daring and blatantly sexual, though always couched in our deceptive cloud of wit. That alone was worth the time we spent on producers, writers and the cast. And thanks to technology, if your patient happened to miss it while it was running, they can easily get all the episodes on whatever device they have and watch them over and over again—further reinforcing our own ideology.

All that I say here is true of games as well. And of course, we provide much more salacious fare than this simple sitcom. The point is, shows like this one present sex in such a lighthearted innocuous but nevertheless alluring fashion to young people—they are quite prepared to move on to the more serious depictions we deliver.

The deleterious effects of entertainment on the human soul are many, from the aforementioned casual attitudes toward sex, to callousness toward human life, to the less significant but more prevalent propensity to find stupidity funny, thereby dulling the sense of any meaningful thought and feeling. A constant diet of violence will have a very strong effect on humans, especially those that are prone to any problematic mental discord. Of course, we always make sure to nudge Americans especially, to invoke the sacrosanct First Amendment Right of Freedom of Speech if anyone approaches a conversation suggesting violence in the media is a factor in the increasing number of crazed individuals who blatantly kill innocent people for no apparent reason. Push the gun restrictions instead. We are on safer ground there because nothing of importance will ever happen in that department, and while they are arguing about it, we can keep producing more and more violent films, TV shows and games.

Nothing pleases us more than the increase in violence both real and imaginary. If we can get the human race to annihilate each other, we will not only have won the war but will also be provided with amusement while we watch it happen. In the meantime, they can get closer to it by entertaining themselves with murder at its most gory.

Excessive entertainment provides several other effects. One is fairly simple and achieved just from getting them to sit down. It is the waste of the limited time the Enemy gives them each day. They forget that they cannot get these hours back. Of course, immoderate time is what you are going to be pushing for. A limited amount of entertainment is *not* very harmful—and in fact probably beneficial for humans—they do need some time to unwind. However, it is easy with the changes in society and technology to turn that into *much* more time. It is the human's natural disposition to increase in time what they begin to spend time doing. In other words, if your man is a reading man, the more he reads the more he will want to read. Whereas if he is a "watching" man (which so very many are), the more he watches, the more he will want to watch. There will always be one more episode or a similar movie that you can push into his mind just as the previous one ends. We have even generated the self-mocking humorous admittance of binge watching among them. Any real shame they may have experienced in the past for such an indulgence is now completely absent. They are almost proud and boastful of the hours spent in complete inanity—as if they were triumphant in some worthy cause!

We have increased our effectiveness by adding little "suggested" titles in whatever app or program they use, thereby bringing their attention to yet another few hours waste of time watching or playing something they didn't even know about but are very happy to have found. You know what I mean, the "*If you liked such and such, you will also like...*" You get the idea: always suggest one more movie, one more game. What helps us in this area is the gregariousness of humans. They love to talk about entertainment as well as watch it. So help him feel like he would be "out of it" if he hasn't seen all the latest movies and TV shows that his friends are talking about. Even if it is something he doesn't really enjoy, the desire to appear to be "with it," will usually be motivation enough for him to watch something. Then the addictive nature of the show will be sufficient to *keep* him watching.

We started this in the 1950's with the so-called "Soap Operas" and ever since then writers have completely embraced the notion of continuous story-telling. We have medical dramas that can move the audience to tears but also include quick sexual encounters in the storage room. We have cliffhanger cop shows that can keep an entire country waiting on the edge of their seats for an episode to air. We have sitcoms that follow the lives of quirky characters over the years.

This has been a marvelous tactic of ours—keep humans wanting to know the rest of the story and you will keep them watching!

Now of course, you are likely thinking, isn't this what writers like Charles Dickens did in the nineteenth century? How is this any different? Well for one thing, even though his stories were published in installments and kept the audience waiting and wanting to know the end, it was very different due to the fact that the people were *reading,* not watching. Reading is usually always what we want to keep humans from doing—unless the work is authored by our side, of course—and there are lots of those today. Reading is a very different act than just watching and listening. One's mind is more engaged while reading because one has to visualize and make sense of the words. That is not the case with watching. Watching is a much more *mind numbing* than a *mind-engaging* activity. So, we advocate watching.

Besides, Dickens of all people, is one that was hostile to our Father, he was far too much in the Enemy's camp—his characters displayed too many moral rights and wrongs for us to risk using work like his, even if the story does draw one in. There is no lack of villains in his work but they are very obviously *portrayed* as villains. We want to promote the kind of villain that is justified in what he does and admired for how well he does bad things. Take that one popular show we pushed a few years ago where the main character would rid the world each season of a killer by murdering them himself. It was enormously popular and viewers applauded his actions, and thanks to clever writing and today's psychology, they rather liked him, the fact that he was a serial killer did not bother them in the least.

Thankfully, the modern world has moved away from reading to such a nice degree that even university students, having entertained themselves almost to death for many years, have a difficult time sitting through an hour's lecture or reading a whole text. I once had a patient (a college student) who was so addicted that I could get him to watch basketball games on his computer during his history class. That is how well in hand we have them.

One of the greatest advantages that Hollywood has given us in this day and age is the tendency to be entertained rather than educated. Not that you won't find a movie or TV show or even YouTube video here and there that has what the Enemy considers a "good" message. Of course, we have to allow that or humans might realize just how firm our control over Hollywood really is. Even so, humans have such a difficult time with moderation that their discrimination between the inspirational and the detrimental is quite useless when it comes to entertainment. We allow the few instances of uplifting or instructive entertainment just so we can keep a preponderance of the degrading and destructive.

The other category of entertainment I need to mention is the inane. This type is easy to promulgate because it is not blatantly violent or sexual, the main ingredient being humor. We have marketed stupidity quite effectively. This entertainment not only wastes copious amounts of time on something worthless, it also promotes vulgarity and crassness that contributes to the overall decline of human character. There is nothing today that we cannot portray as humorous: sex, bodily functions, foolishness, conceit, ignorance, prejudice, dull-mindedness and even cruelty. This type of entertainment is the opposite of anything that in the Enemy's eyes is virtuous, charitable, refined, cultured or intelligent and its effect on society is massively deleterious, though largely unrecognized. It also helps enormously in the deterioration of language department that we are diligently working on. Soon we will have produced a language that is so limited in its vocabulary with words so meaningless that the communication of essential truths (again according to the Enemy) will be virtually impossible. Terms that do not even make sense in the English language as they are presently used (such as "be like") will supersede their really important words like faith and grace— indeed they already have!

Best,
Wormwood

The Green Road

My Dear Tempters,

If your patient is a real, sincere believer that will readily dismiss the claims of disbelievers, then try to manipulate his conception of the Enemy instead. Move him away from what is written in their dreary scriptures, and turn his mental idea of God into that appealing but quite lopsided image of him as a kind and accepting God who loves him no matter what he does or thinks. Your patients will base this one-sided view very literally on their own set of doctrinal statements about him. What humans do not realize is they are very much inclined to create an image and idea of their Christian god that is as comfortable and convenient as they can make him. They adjust and stretch his teachings until they become broad enough to encompass every kind of behavior they find enjoyable or cannot seem to control.

One approach in recent years (in fact a new spin on an old ploy) is what we like to call "The Green Road" or more explicitly the "customization of religious sensibilities." Simply put, this has the effect of helping your patients make religion comfortable and affordable. Now of course, by affordable, I do not mean the elimination of tithing or donations, I mean it in its figurative sense. For real religious conviction, there is a price to be paid. Much has to be sacrificed for real faith, of the kind that the Enemy's most ardent followers speak. It is sometimes a hardship to pay, though his followers, who *have* paid it, count it as nothing compared to what they receive. (So they say... though I can hardly credit it). What we have pushed in recent years is the notion that one can keep one's faith and not have to pay quite so much.

One of the Enemy's best soldiers in the middle of the last century, whose voice we went to great pains to silence during our happy time known as World War II, coined the term, "Cheap Grace."[*] He thus brought to the attention of many Christians their mistaken notion that benefitting from Christ's grace required no cost, no broken or contrite heart, and only an intellectual assent was necessary to secure forgiveness. Luckily that realization did NOT sweep the Christian world and we have many denominations and individuals back in the saddle of what they believe is an easy ride to redemption. It is just this particular notion—that His grace *ought* to be cheap and not so costly—which we want instilled in them. They inevitably fall back on the idea—correct in one sense but not in another—that because Christ paid for their sins, they do not have to. So they go from the correct understanding that Christ paid because they *could* not, to Christ paid *so I don't need to do anything* other than accept that fact. In other words, we want them thinking they can make adjustments in their day-to-day living, disregarding a commandment here, bending another there, altering their conception of others, until they have created their own little independent religious world that keeps them comfortable and completely at ease in the lifestyle they *really* want to lead.

The brilliant part about it is we help them create the completely false illusion that their own personal relationship with God is as strong as ever. We whisper that for *them*, this life has His complete sanction and approval, regardless of what the rest of their fellow church members might think or say. And do keep them focused on *that* idea—what their neighbors think—that will bring all sorts of other problems. They themselves *know* (and will emphatically state) that this is what *real* religion is, not those outward behaviors that have been imposed upon them from formal religious institutions.

What makes this possible is our ability to direct their focus on one truth, and by so doing, block out other truths. Since that seminal moment long ago in *the* Garden, that has always been our advantage. Telling a truth to push a lie. Their belief in the truth is what makes

---

[*] Dietrich Bonhoeffer, *The Cost of Discipleship*, (New York, 1959), 43.

it so effective. In the case of customized religion, it *is* the truth that God loves them. God *does* love them, no matter what they choose, no matter what they do, no matter how low they sink, no matter what others think of them—he loves them. By pushing his love they are able to believe that his love abrogates his law. *We* know it does not, but we can get them to believe it does. With our suggestions, they get the idea that love and law are sometimes mutually exclusive, when that is far from the case. So telling themselves that God loves them, they quietly disregard one covenant and promise after another, still secure in his love and effectively cutting themselves off from his power and promise of redemption.

This reasoning, that religion and God in their lives should not make them feel bad about themselves or uneasy or burdened when they want enjoyment, is such a delightful thing to watch unfold. Man in his natural state inclines toward ease—not effort—in thinking, eating, and physical exertion in every aspect of life. For most people, the physical demands of life are much more easily obtained than they have been in ages past (i.e., getting food and shelter, etc.), and if it *is* not yet easier, then the quest for ease is paramount. It is simple to transfer that physical *life of ease* desire to their spiritual life as well. Help them start asking themselves the following: "Why should their relationship with deity cause them guilt, discomfort or uneasiness? Why can't one be close to him in a way that resonates personally, rather than in the old-fashioned, church-going way? Why would he impose outdated commandments? Doesn't God really love them as they are, with their own particular predispositions? Without living a bunch of arbitrary and old-fashioned rules probably thought up by men anyway?" Tell them it is not God who brings this guilt and accountability; it is today's religious culture and judgmental fanatics.

If you do a little research into the archives you will see how we effectively used this philosophy in the so-called "Sexual Revolution" we pushed in the 1960s. What we suggested (and that is *all* we had to do, thanks again to what I have mentioned above—man's natural propensities) was that all this angst about human sexuality was merely imposed on society from antiquated religious ideology and they were far better off being free from these unnatural fetters. Sexuality was natural; it was normal—we obligingly suggested. So believing us, the greater part of society has effectively disregarded any and all limitations to sexuality. The poor animals hardly realize how blind they were and they are consequently now *less* free and more obsessed and captive than ever. Religious restraints on human intimacy were thus a casualty of the revolution.

Anyway, back to my point. Help them ask themselves these questions about whether the real God that they have come to know loves them no matter what they do, and then give them the answer: "Of course he does! He will never love you less just because you stop attending church," etc. The truth of the Enemy's love will mask the lie that what they choose to *do* does not matter. In any other aspect of life they would recognize the falsehood. Take education for example. Would they want their children to have the kind of teacher that just praised their students *for being in class* and didn't worry about whether they made the effort to learn to read or write? No correction on grammar or spelling? No Math exams (*that* causes stress!). No consequences for late homework; in fact, why even give homework? So the teacher completely eliminates anything that might affect feelings of contentedness and comfort. Obviously, no parent would want their child to have a teacher that asked nothing of them, other than to acknowledge they *were* the teacher and they cared for the students.

What kind of employer would have no deadlines, standards of work or company policies to follow? What kind of nutritionist would advocate eating anything that tasted good, in any amount? What kind of coach would ask nothing of their players other than to play in whatever way they thought best at any particular time? In no other facet of life would they really advocate ease and pleasure, rather than hard work, effort, sacrifice and improvement. And yet in the area of spirituality (that word has less historical baggage than religion by the way, so use that), we have such an easy time convincing them that all guilt, all difficulties, and all feelings of falling short should be erased completely and religion should be personalized by merely consisting of feeling satisfied and contented with knowing God loves them.

This is yet another example of how humans can so easily pick and choose what parts of their scriptural record they want to believe or live and ignore the others. In this instance, our Enemy's injunction that "whoever saves his life will lose it, and whoever loses his life will save it" is quietly omitted. So don't allow them to pause on those particular verses if they happen to be reading. In taking the easy road they are in fact clinging most tenaciously to "their" life. It is the hard, uphill, uncomfortable road, the letting go of "their" life that leads to the Enemy's wretched eternal life. They are under the delusion that his road can be adjusted so it is not quite so steep and rocky. But in fact, as soon as they do adjust it, they are off the road itself and into the gentle downward sloping, grass covered easy path. Hence the designation, "The Green Road." It is soft and relaxing, cool and gratifying, the perfect anodyne for any difficulty. Suggest they take off their shoes!

Best,
Wormwood

Every Day Is Judgment Day

Dear Tempters,

I need to give you some guidance in the area of judging. This can be more complex than one would suppose. You need to understand some basic principles about the whole notion of judgment. Humans judge numerous things every day: what is the best way to drive to work, which school should I send my children to, whether a particular movie is worth my time, etc. We try to sway them to ignore commandments and rationalize the negative impact of their poor choices, but we also use the argument, in certain instances, that they are *"being too judgmental."* The Enemy actually wants them to judge for themselves a great deal, despite his words (which they often misuse or misunderstand—more of that in a minute). If they are trying to be good disciples they will need to judge between good and evil *all the time.* And they do so not only with his sanction but also—despite our best efforts—with his *help!* Suffice it to say, humans are supposed to judge and much of that judgment involves other people.

For example, a mother must decide whether she will allow her fourteen-year-old daughter to spend the night at a friend's house, even though it is obvious that the friend's standards are not what hers are. A middle-aged married man has to decide whether to accept a lunch invitation with a very friendly female co-worker whose cleavage is showing. Now these judgments will be connected to our valuable work by extension if we can get them focused on the Enemy's *"Judge not that ye be not judged"* admonition. If we can persuade them that there should be no boundaries or restrictions on their behavior based on *"not judging,"* then we have a large foot in the door of their actions. "Go out to lunch with the young gregarious office worker," we tell him, "otherwise you are being judgmental about her and how she dresses—you will make her feel judged!" To the mother of the fourteen-year-old, we send the message that of course her daughter should be friends with everyone! If not, then she is teaching her daughter to be judgmental, and isn't that in direct conflict with what Jesus taught?

Thus, we can get them to whittle away the safety and standards that the Enemy wants them to keep—all in the guise of trying not to judge others. You see, our goal here is to get them in the most vulnerable situation possible, and they will—by their choices—eventually get there. You will likely have noticed that they have a hard time with moderation and wisdom—especially the young people. Observe what strides we have taken with society as a whole. Behaviors that used to be considered wrong by the majority of the populace are now *not only* completely accepted by the majority, but those people who still believe in the right and wrong about them are labeled as judgmental, prejudiced, narrow-minded and self-righteous. Oh, we have made great inroads here! "*Judge not*" has been one of our most effective devices.

Having said that, another and sometimes far more powerful approach to the judgment issue is the flip side. When humans understand and accept that they *must* make some judgments in regard to one another in order to maintain their beliefs and standards, what we do then is to focus the judgment on the individuals themselves rather than certain behavior. The thing about the actual process of judgment, when it comes to humans, can be understood if we look at a funerary ritual of the ancient Egyptians. I know this seems odd as an explanation, but bear with me. The Egyptians believed that the deceased went through a ritual after death that was called, "*The Weighing of the Heart.*" In the imagery accompanying the religious texts, they showed the deceased's heart put on a scale and weighed against the feather or figure of the goddess *Maat* who represented Truth and Justice. A person's heart had to weigh the same in order to be received into eternity with Osiris.

Well, the point for us here is that humans *do not know* each other's hearts—they only know outward actions. So they can never be involved in the "weighing" or the "judgment" of others. They *are not* Truth and Justice. Only the Enemy really knows each heart and that is why it is his prerogative to judge. He will be the ultimate judge unless we can somehow circumvent the whole wretched process—which we desperately hope to do eventually—but I digress. When humans judge one another they do not know all there is to know and so that is why they have been warned about judging each other. They do not have the "whole story."

For example, perhaps your patient's neighbor just got word that her son has cancer. That is why she backed out of the driveway without seeing his car behind her. As your patient slams on his brakes and verbally lashes out at the neighbor, he can have no idea what is happening in her heart—instead he has decided she is not only a lousy driver but also a typical "blond!" We do so love stereotyping. Or suppose your patient has not seen a friend at church for a while, she will make the determination that her friend has not only lost her faith but is likely out on the lake on Sunday rather than being in church. Now whether or not her friend has a viable reason for being absent from church or really *is* at the lake, is not the point. The point is for your patients to set themselves up as *Maat*—as Truth and Justice. Whether she has truth/facts, i.e., she saw her friend leaving her home in the car pulling the boat, or whether she is just making assumptions, does not matter to us. What matters is that instead of loving her friend she is judging her friend and thinking less of her as she does it. Even a fleeting thought in the mind is a good start. You can then develop it from there into some good gossip and eventually cold distance.

We have done a great deal of work by encouraging humans to stand as judges for each other. History is rife with our favorite stories of mistreatment, exploitation and abuse of others in the guise of religious devotion. For some reason, these people find it difficult to live the Enemy's commandments and try to help others to do so, without condemning them at the same time. The fear of the "other" that lives differently is inherent in their relationships both in their own neighborhood and the world at large. When the Enemy exhorts humans to love him *and* their neighbors, they do not always see the connection between the two commandments. Once they begin to realize that the more they love him, the *easier* it will be to love their neighbor, then our cause is in danger! So rather than focus on loving him *and* their neighbor, we try to get them to focus on whether *their neighbor* (in their humble opinion) loves the Enemy and obeys him. That was *not* what he said, but our job is to make them think that loving their neighbor revolves around making sure their neighbor is keeping the Enemy's commandments.

Humans have a propensity to build themselves up (at least in their own minds) by pulling one another down. They can't help themselves. If you can get your patient to notice people struggling with commandments that they themselves don't struggle with, you can utilize this inclination to your benefit. It rarely occurs to them that they have an easier time seeing the faults of others than their own. So the kind of judging we want to promote here are those judgments that focus on other individuals—individuals that are judged by comparison and not by what is in their heart—because they don't and *cannot fully* know that only the Enemy can. What the Enemy wants is for the good man in the office to know that he ought not to go to lunch with the sleezebucket coworker (excuse my colloquial—I don't mean to judge—but really did you see how short that skirt was?) but to realize that he does not know everything about her and why she acts and dresses the way she does. So he has used judgment about not going to lunch but he has reserved another kind of pointed, focused judgment about her *personally*—because he knows she is a child of the Enemy and is loved by him. *That* is what we are trying to fight *against*—both kinds of effectual judgment—what the Enemy would call "righteous" judgment. If we can't get him to go to lunch with her and put himself in danger of other sins, we at least want him to think less of her and condemn her in his mind—eventually to the point of snide remarks to other co-workers. Do you grasp the essentials here? Push for a judgment as long as it benefits our goals. Either persuade them to harshly judge others in the name of religion, or have them refrain from any balanced judgment that may keep them safe from other temptations we might offer. We always advocate the extreme ends of the spectrum.

Best,
Wormwood

Fig Leaves Are Always in Fashion

My Dear Tempters,

I must bring to your attention a point upon which some of you are quibbling and by so doing wasting precious time. It is the use to which we can put the natural feelings of guilt that arise when humans violate the Enemy's laws. Remember these laws fall into two categories: acts of commission, or those of omission—both are important. First of all, you need to understand a concept that we have successfully used for a long time: replace "guilt" with "shame."

You have been arguing among yourselves because some of you mistakenly believe that the words are synonymous, and I must inform you that they are not. Understand that the distinction I make here is ours and not the Enemy's. He often uses the two synonymously, but for our purposes, we use them differently. Guilt is something that has been with us since that faraway time and place called by the Enemy, the *Garden of Eden*. We have persuaded most of the world that this is just a myth, though little do they know that it was an actual place, and what happened there is of utmost importance. It was the scene of one of our father's most powerful triumphs—and to date the one with the most long-lasting consequences. *

In the Garden, our father was able to entice the first humans to transgress one of the Enemy's commandments—thus guilt entered upon the human stage. Now, we believe that the Enemy actually wants his children to feel guilt when they do something wrong. For him, guilt is similar to the body's nervous system—sending a signal of pain when an arm is broken. The pain will make him aware of the break and motivate him to get it fixed. That is most dangerous for us! We do not want humans going to the Enemy when they feel

36

guilt. He will most surely help them recover from it by that odious repentance process so freely available to them at all times. True guilt causes humility and an awareness of the need for cleansing. Of course, humans must first be cognizant of both the guilt and the need for cleansing. This is where you come in.

One thing that we have found to be most effective in this area is to replace guilt with shame. Here is the difference between them: guilt is based on the awareness that one has fallen short of what they ought to be, and has disappointed the Enemy. It is focused on his laws and his love—both his love for them and theirs for him. Shame, on the other hand, is focused entirely on the human. Guilt says to him, "You have done something wrong (law) and offended God (love)."** It is the behavior that needs to be changed. Shame says to him, "You are a terrible person, how could you have done that?" Shame keeps the focus on *him* rather than the sin. (This approach, by the way, works for everything from gossip to adultery.) Shame creates the feeling that there is no hope of ever changing because the problem is inherent in the person, rather than the behavior. Shame avoids both the law and love of the Enemy and keeps all the attention on the sinner.

Guilt is actually very effectual for humans when it is properly understood. Shame keeps them wallowing in recurring cycles of sin and engenders self-pity and spiritual inertia. Rather than recognizing true guilt for what it is, they slowly fall into the deep depression of shame and cannot extricate themselves. With a little help from our side, they are all too willing to jump into the pit of infamy and disgrace. When they are in that state, there is *so* much we can do, twisting and turning and relentlessly pulling them further down. True guilt is a difficult state for us to work with as it will move men up toward the Enemy.

So above all things turn the guilt into shame. Shame will lean toward hypocrisy and duplicity in order to keep the knowledge of the transgression from others. True guilt will want the remedy that requires a painful acknowledgment. Distract them from reading or pondering on the Enemy, or any of those dismal stories of his followers that came to understand repentance and forgiveness. Keep them away from individuals who have overcome similar struggles and could help them. Encourage them to play the comparison game— you know what I mean—telling themselves that nobody else struggles with this sin or habit like they do. Nobody else has such a hard time overcoming it. Nobody understands. Those thoughts are again pointed inward. Or concentrate on the inevitable worry that everyone *knows*. Everyone is judging them. Avoid anything that comes even close to humility or meekness and especially any willingness to change. Guilt will motivate change. Shame is too indolent and sluggish to change.

This notion can best be illustrated if you consider what happened in the garden after our father enticed the man and woman. They knew they had transgressed the Enemy's law, hence the realization of their "nakedness." It was *our* suggestion to have them make some fig leaves to cover themselves. We wanted them shamed and hiding from the Enemy. And we thought things were going well for a while—that is, until the Enemy *himself* made coats of skin and covered them! So we have now learned something important: keep them in fig leaves and away from the Enemy and his clothes!

You can comprehend why if you think about the difference between the fig leaves and clothing made of skins—both literally and figuratively. First of all, it was the man and woman trying (without much success) to clothe *themselves*, as opposed to being clothed by one who knew and loved them. Humans cannot cover themselves— it is not possible—though they will inevitably try. They cannot, of themselves, take away that state of nakedness—the Enemy must do it for them. Secondly, fig leaves are quite inadequate for the purpose, *and* will certainly not last long.

Coats of skins are warm and soft and durable and will likely make them feel the Enemy's love, enough to initiate a desire to change. This metaphoric difference can provide a model as to how we proceed. We offer fig leaves for all sins, misdemeanors, and petty problems. "Cover it up quickly," we say. "This will do the job nicely, and no one need ever know." Fig leaves are easy to obtain—no effort required—and they are lighter and less confining than animal skins, so humans needn't bother with the Enemy at all. Today's fig leaves come in an almost endless variety: distracting entertainment, mind numbing drugs, soul-sucking pornography and, most popular of all, placing the blame on everyone and everything but themselves. Whatever fig leaf they try, soon the reality of the "naked" soul under sin (which the fig leaf has done nothing for) will continue to generate the shame we want to nurture. Keep them from the Enemy and *his* "clothing" for it will only lead them *away* from our influence.

Best,
Wormwood

* There are some of us who fear that our Father might have miscalculated and not quite comprehended the entire garden experience (though keep that to yourselves for now), we know of some humans who actually revere the first man and woman for their courage, rather than condemning them—if you can believe it? But, it is just that sort of thing that makes me a bit worried about the whole business.

** I assume that you all realize when I use the pronouns "he/him," etc., I mean males and females. I am certainly not going to be influenced in my e-mails by the silly gender war with words we have instigated among these foolish humans. Even though it is such a delightful example of how we take their focus off what is important—in this case, treating women equally—and turn it to what will not make any difference at all, in this case, altering language. Men who do not respect women will not change their attitude by using words like "chairperson." The problem was not the language in the first place. Ah, the beauty of distraction!

SILLY WOMEN SYNDROME

My Dear Tempters,

One of the greatest inroads we have made to date is what I like to call, the *Silly Women Syndrome.* Ironically, I take that title from something one of the Enemy's able soldiers wrote many years ago. In cautioning the people of dangers to come (it seems they are annoyingly aware of what we are going to try even before *we* do!), he gave a long list of our favorite sins and then warned that this sort would creep into houses and lead captive silly women, and then something or other about divers lusts. At the time we were apprehensive that women would be conscious of exactly what we were trying to do with them. And, I think for a long time they were—as it has been women who have been more naturally inclined to remain virtuous and morally strong. Typically, they have been harder targets for our sexual sin attacks and they have had an undeniable influence on men, helping them to fight against their natural inclinations.

I am now happy to report that for the first time in centuries we have been able to do just what was described so long ago—on a widespread scale, mind you! One of our most joyous victories has been the twentieth century's two-front attack that simultaneously focused on women and morality. Humans refer to these famous battles (which we were behind, though they seem to take all the credit—as if it was a victory *for* them!) as Women's Liberation and the Sexual Revolution. By ingeniously putting these two together, we have been able to quite literally "creep into houses and lead away silly women." The humor for us comes from the sheer blindness of referring to what has happened as liberation, when in reality it is captivity... as that interfering Paul described so accurately. There is no need to worry, by the way, that our work will be recognized as a fulfillment as most people do not read his words anymore, and if they do, they are temporized and adjusted to fit current standards of morality.

Of course, it is true that we had to give up one of our time-honored avenues of conquest in order to bring this to pass. What I mean here is the total dominance of men over women. Oh yes, that was our idea as well—certainly not the Enemy's! He has esteemed women from the beginning, but for centuries, we were able to convince men that women should be controlled and restrained and that they were not equals. Indeed, in past centuries, we had men believing that women were the source of much evil. We even had them convinced that this was a God-given view. Their misunderstanding of the events in that garden long ago was the basis of our twisting the truth. But now seeing the state of things, I believe it has been worth it for men to "allow" women freedom and choice because we have been able to blind so many women as to who they really are, and what is important. The consequence of pulling moral restraints from women has been far greater than for men.

You see, one of the keys here was the "creeping into houses" for we knew if we could pull women out of their homes by telling them they would never be equal with men if they did not *do* what men *do*, then the rest would be easy. The poor fools, in their minds, "equality" was synonymous with "sameness," when in reality it is nothing of the sort. To this day they do not realize being respected by men is not dependent on whether they are in the home or out of it, working as a fireman or a waitress, raising a child or heading a corporation—but rather on men coming to value them for who they are instead of viewing them as mere sexual objects. It was always men that needed to wake up to that, not women! Though even now, with their so-called equality, we can still get a great many men to treat them as inferior and/or merely sexual beings. (The proliferation of pornography has helped immensely.)

Women have always been capable of anything—from leading a country, to writing a masterpiece of literature—and we have had to give up the whole repression business as society (in most of the world but certainly not all at this point) has finally come to that conclusion. But in the process, as women have taken control of their lives, they have given up virtue as well. By including the ideology of sexual freedom concurrently with women's liberation, we have "silly women" not only leaving their houses, but leaving all moral restraint as well. Women are now as delightfully vulgar and promiscuous as men ever were. The icing on the cake is what has been left in these houses—children! We knew that if we could get wives and mothers in our chains, we would have the next generation captive. And to our delight, that is exactly what has happened! In their desperate quest for equality, they have looked in all the wrong places (see my Selfie-Esteem e-mail on this). Leaving behind the strength that virtue gave them, they are now easy targets and their children just fall into our hands, for no one is at home to teach them right from wrong, strength from weakness and truth from error.

If you remember my first e-mail and the analogy of the spider's web, you will see how well that illustrates the *Silly Women Syndrome.* By searching for validation in a job or education or fitness (and the list goes on), they miss the boat entirely as to their real worth and what their purpose in life is, and at the same time make themselves vulnerable to an almost limitless number of other strands of the sticky web—most important—immorality. That is why the Women's Liberation and the Sexual Revolution go hand in hand—they feed on each other. I am happy to report that real fulfillment and joy have become even more elusive to them even in the midst of their hard won "equality!"

I am also happy to report that the old notion of women as sexual objects has experienced resurgence rather than decline, *despite* the assertion of equal rights. We enjoy the fact that most women are quite baffled at this—again—look for pornography as a key factor. The women who participate it its production don't seem to mind the inconsistency. (I must say it surprises even us, skilled tempters!)

So in your work, make sure you direct your women to focus on their sexuality, their bodies, how they are being treated, what they are wearing, how young and sexy they appear, how many men they can attract, how, like men, they can be in their accomplishments, their speech and behavior— their careers, their self-esteem *anything* but an emphasis on the innate female nature that was always intended by the Enemy to be different. Plant in their hearts the false notion mentioned above, that equality means there should be no differences. Convince them that as long as they are in control, they can be viewed as a sexual object and it is acceptable because *they* are calling the shots now. You will see how many will actually focus their major efforts on just that—their appearance as a sexual being. Few of them see it as the step backward that it is. They are content to be that object. Few of them consider the history of women, or if they do they misunderstand both the problems and the solutions. Avoid *any* tendencies toward real selfless service, home, family and a virtuous life built upon moral principles.

Continue the good work we have done in making a woman who stays at home and has children appear ignorant and unaccomplished, dull-minded and out of touch, wasting her talents and stifling her creativity with the mundane and unfulfilling realities of child-rearing. What helps us here is the difficulty humans have in seeing the whole picture—in this case, the potential of a human and a mother's role in that potential. The "myopic motherhood view" sees only the fact that she spends all her time meeting everyone else's needs while her own remain unfulfilled. The comparison approach functions well here. Working women, especially those that are financially prosperous, usually dress very well, have nice vehicles and exude all the trappings of worldly success. Put them in the way of the more limited income mother who is tired of the ubiquitous laundry and can't afford a pedicure. Most of all, promote the idea that to have any self-worth, they must adopt a philosophy of moral relativism and the "liberation" of self.

One last point here: there is the flip side of this women's issue. Simply put, it is the woman whom we tempt in another way. These are the ones who really *do* value the role of wife and mother and yet because of circumstances, have not been able to have either. With these, we try and promote the "Waiting Game" which is just what it says—we want them to wait for good things (i.e., husband, children) to come to them and do nothing substantial for themselves or others *while* they wait. Because they put motherhood first, we can talk them out of any real effort in education or career or service. They feel the need to wait *until...* you get the picture.

Just help them brush aside ambition, determination or discipline and bring in the injustice and the subsequent wallowing. Don't let them see or feel the inherent potential to "mother" those around them. Don't allow a vision of the Enemy's promises kept in some future place. Keep any Abrahamic faith pushed down, ridiculed or spent. And for badness' sake, don't let them see or hear from any *real* examples of women who have overcome the "Waiting Game" and gone on to live heroic lives. They are out there—I assure you. And they are often *far* more effective against our work than the others who didn't have to wait.

Best,
Wormwood

Knowest Not

My Dear Tempters,

I have heard some criticism of my practice of including ideas from the Enemy's own words to humans in my advice to you. Imbeciles! It is paramount that we are aware of what he is teaching. How else can we develop strategies to best counter it, I would like to know? Sometimes you are so naïve! I will continue to use his words in my advice for attack, so expect it!

I want to discuss something he said through that loathsome John in his book that allegedly reveals what will happen in the future. We are not certain how much reliance we can put on what is said— not that we really comprehend it anyway, and at any rate very few actually read the book these days, and those who do are apt to draw the wrong conclusions and run about in useless endeavors such as collecting guns or waiting to be "raptured."

Anyway, back to the subject in this book, the Enemy chastises the people for being lukewarm and then tells them that they think they are rich and have need of nothing and, *"knowest not that thou are wretched, and miserable, and poor, and blind, and naked."** The next statement is even worse as he tells them how they can stop being miserable and poor and blind, etc. My point here is that we try our best to keep humans utterly unaware of their real state, for the very lack of self-knowledge will prevent making any significant changes. We *try* to keep them wretched, miserable, poor, blind, and naked.

You may ask how a person could think they were rich and in need of nothing and not know that they were poor and wretched.

---

* Revelation 3:17

45

Well, the fact is, what the Enemy was saying here was the state of the person's soul—not his literal physical state of affairs—though that often enters into the equation. This is a message about spiritual blindness and poverty. We *always* try to turn humans to the material world and keep them away from their spiritual selves. They can easily exist in a state of spiritual numbness while busily engaged in daily pursuits that have very little meaning in reality and none in eternity. While achieving financial prosperity, they are impoverished in matters of the spirit. We want them in this vulnerable state because it will cause a spiritual starvation they will hardly recognize, though undoubtedly some are more perceptive than others and can feel this wretchedness. If you are not careful in your work, they may not only become aware of their real state, but worse yet, try to do something about it.

Humans have a propensity—which we have cultivated—to be self-blind, to be blissfully unaware of their own folly and neglect. They are quick to scrutinize others around them and focus on limitations and mistakes (or view them with envy), but they are less inclined to see the reality of their own circumstances. Sometimes that little annoying thing they call "conscience" will push its way to the surface of thought, bringing light to the eyes and a cognizance to the mind. But, don't despair; with our help they have become quite adept at pushing it ruthlessly back down—burying it under hard work or busyness, or more often than not, entertainment. You want to avoid allowing them to see things as they really are. Consciousness of the state of their heart and mind (the real state, mind you—not the false, dressed up one we promote), is the danger point from which you must push back. We want blindness. If we can't have that, we at least want sand in the eyes. So above all, keep them away from those humans who *do* see. Though there are presently only a few of them, they have apparently made themselves invulnerable to our attacks.

The "nakedness" mentioned is another thing we try our hardest to prevent them from apprehending. Naked in this sense implies absolute humiliating honesty before the Enemy. (See more on this in my Fig Leaves e-mail). It means being seen by him with all their evil deeds and thoughts, their flaws and petty little selfishness—a state they would discredit, even if they were told. None of them want that, they shrink from it and wish to be covered (with fig leaves...), yet they *are* naked before him. That is where we want them—content with fig leaves, rather than desiring the kind of clothing that the Enemy has in mind for them, clothing that has been washed white as he describes it. That only comes with change. They must allow him to clothe them, and you want them either satisfied in their nakedness or unaware of it.

Repentance is what the Enemy is talking about—though we have been able quite successfully to make that word resonate with images of bigoted, religious fanatics. So much so that many humans now treat the whole notion with amused contempt. Don't let your patient get near it! Be careful, for when they begin to spend their time and concentrate their attention on the Enemy and his work, then you need to get in there immediately and turn them elsewhere. You must keep them from any quiet time spent in pondering their present condition relative to their Maker. Keep the music on, add more channels on cable, and present a new electronic device (Pokémon Go, perhaps?) Anything that will keep them from the stark realization that they may indeed "have it all" by the world's standards and yet feel empty—"lukewarm," the Enemy called it.

Always remember, humans will hesitate on the threshold of change, so if you can, get them to believe that it would be almost impossible, too painful, or simply too difficult to go forward. The Enemy will reward even their feeblest efforts so it is best to keep them in this indeterminate state. In case they move *to* the threshold, keep them there or better yet, have them back away from what will seem an insuperable task. Don't worry if they sit there for a long time *on* the threshold, contemplating the task ahead, as long as they never cross it and actually begin.

Best,
Wormwood

THE DULL EDGE OF THE BLADE

My Dear Tempters,

A nother significant achievement of ours in these modern days has been the promotion of what I call dull-mindedness. What I mean by that term is a fairly constant state of mental torpor, laziness, or inertia, an inability to focus deeply and/or at any length on important concepts. Now I know what you are thinking: don't we have a great number of universities and institutions of higher learning and scientists, etc.? Well, yes of course, though we are hard at work with that particular group through other avenues. There are plenty of individuals whose minds have not only been trained but are keen or even brilliant. That is not what I am referring to here. What I mean is the average human being who is perfectly capable of rational and critical thinking but who has let us—through various means—dull the sharp edges of his mind to the point that he lives entirely on the surface of thought.

Mental laziness will never be able to comprehend the Enemy. The mind must be engaged as well as the heart in that process (which, I must add, we do not fully comprehend, though we still try to prevent it). Consequently, we attack both the mind and the heart. The dulled edge of a sword will never cut anything. It can never defend but must always be a useless appendage. The Enemy wants a mind sharp and engaged; we want it dull and languorous.

Our methodology here is to feed the minds of humans, food ("for thought" as they say?) that barely keeps the brain functioning and significantly underused. The best tactic is entertainment. I have addressed that in an earlier e-mail—read it again and apply the principles here. The inane entertainment of the contemporary world requires very little mental exertion. Thus, like the muscles of a leg in a cast for weeks, the brain becomes atrophied. If we can keep feeding it more and more entertainment, the brain's capacity—and I should add—inclination for hard work, will be significantly diminished.

You can see this in action with the increased decline in reading. Oh, I don't mean popular novels and such—those are weapons from our own arsenal for the most part. You will notice that there are few people today reading the novels of the last few centuries—they are too difficult for them to understand. So even though bookstores and online formats are booming, the greatest part of the material is sordid entertainment, rather than the kind of deep literature of the past that had meaningful messages. This kind of "light" reading can be lumped with games, movies and TV shows, as it does not take much mental effort to comprehend the unrealistic characters, paltry plot or sensational story line. Always push the type of entertainment that utilizes imagery on a screen. The more they indulge in that, the less receptive their minds will be on the serious things of the Enemy. And just think of the screen availability for today's humans—it is beyond our wildest dreams!

The mind can only focus on one thing at a time, despite humans thinking otherwise. So while "glued" to a screen, only the immediate sensations of what is being watched are present and will certainly push out anything else. Notice this effect when children are trying to get their parents' attention in the middle of a movie, or the reverse with a parent trying to talk with their teenager who is deep into a computer game. The comatose persona prevails. With a constant diet of this frail mental engagement, the mind slowly loses its natural capacity for effort and endurance. Furthermore, we have the phenomenon of mental repetition and reiteration, which follows entertainment. The mind will replay the scenes from the movie (sometimes ad nauseam—to our delight!), so that we get additional chances to thrust out any constructive thought or more important ideas. The result of this kind of lengthened attack is that when a patient is required to utilize his mind, the weakened thought process gives up after the very briefest exertion. That is where we want them, back to the comfortable, easy chair of being entertained. Critical thinking is what we want to avoid.

One important work along this line is to keep them busy. We have most humans to the point that they actually feel guilty if they are just sitting and thinking—which is quite amusing as they don't have the same thought about sitting and watching a movie. This is related to another subject (too lengthy for this e-mail, so wait for another one), the fear and dread of silence. But in this context of dull-mindedness, we have them well in hand by providing sound and imagery on a constant basis. Notice the screens at the checkout counters at Wal-Mart or the loud music in the mall. They pride themselves on multitasking and having "too much to do" but don't realize they have let their minds become so slack that everything now has to be "dumbed-down" in order to be comprehended. Their mercurial nature will make them believe busyness is equated with self-development and growth.

We have help in this department with social media sharing. It is easy for the masses to occupy hours in what I call "skim and adopt." They skim through the myriads of shared mindlessness on the Internet, without any kind of analytical or interpretive assessment (because that takes too much mental effort, you see?) and jump on the bandwagon of opinion or belief by adopting a particular idea or viewpoint. We have been able to influence millions of people with blatantly false information by virtue of it being Google-fed to them. Facebook is particularly effective in this realm. Even if you cannot get your patients to believe anything they skim (they don't really read closely or study intently), you have been able to waste many a precious hour at the very least. You also have the advantage of feeding them digested information.

We started this concept long ago. Reader's Digest Condensed Books was one of our good moments in the 1950s and 1960s. We persuaded people that wanted to read, that they really did not have much time to devote to it, so someone else would read ("digest") a book and eliminate portions that the reader could do without. Nobody ever stopped to wonder just whose opinion determined which parts *could* be skipped! They never asked. It was easier to "get through a book" this way. Real literature speaks to the very souls of humans, and it speaks to individuals in different ways. By condensing and distributing to the masses, we could make them think they were still engaged with literature but have it spoon-fed to them. Cliff Notes is another one of our great creations—just enough to get by.

Well, we are essentially doing the same thing with blogs and Facebook posts and the Wikipedia world. Someone else is doing the real reading and thinking instead of them. They are adopting someone else's thoughts, ideas, opinions, beliefs, tastes, habits, words, trends, and recipes. Now you may argue that *good* thoughts, ideas, opinions, beliefs, etc., might be adopted. That is true—and we hope to prevent that by making the destructive thoughts, ideas, opinions and beliefs, etc., more appealing. But the salient point here is that this "skim and adopt" is just one more way to keep the mind lazy. By adopting the thoughts, ideas, opinions and beliefs, etc., of others, you never generate any of your own. So then when you are confronted with difficult doctrinal questions about the Enemy, you retreat into the languor of what you have "skimmed and adopted" rather than go through the spiritual and mental effort to really understand for yourself. That kind of loose and lazy disciple is much easier to persuade to our side. So do your best to lead them down the gentle slope of mental laziness and the dull edge of intellectual indolence.

Best,
Wormwood

THE KNOT OF KNOWLEDGE

My Dear Tempters,

One front of our war is the attack on the acquisition of knowledge. When I speak of knowledge I refer to that real understanding of the truths of the Enemy; given by him, advanced by him, essential to his plan, and understood through his light and power—what he calls wisdom. That kind of knowledge we keep from our patients, that kind of knowledge we are at war with. Of course, the separation of the two (knowledge and wisdom) has been our first offensive move. Knowledge, understood in a singular sense, becomes merely a collection of facts—a collection that is never synthesized. According to the Enemy, wisdom is the application of knowledge or what is considered *his* truth. Hence, we circulate the idea that "scientific" knowledge has absolutely no connection to the Enemy.

Take the idea of the creation of the world. Instead of grasping what the Enemy was trying to tell the humans with the story from Genesis, a story transmitted in the language and the culture of the ancient world, man has tried hard to reconcile the original account with modern scientific understanding of the age of the world and evolution, etc. and has failed. This was one of our great triumphs of the nineteenth century and men like Darwin and Lyell were our unwitting allies. Religious men were at their wit's end scrambling for ways to either dismiss the increasing amount of scientific evidence or to harmonize the seeming disparate accounts. The trouble was, they weren't disparate accounts—they were only being explained in different imagery to different audiences. The vehicle used to present the Enemy's message is fluid and flexible but humans mistake the vehicle for the message itself. Men thought they *had* to reconcile the biblical and the scientific and it was completely unnecessary.

The Enemy wants the creation understood as *his work*—the means and motifs for that understanding are not as important and can be expressed in various ways. So now, the tale is being told in scientific terms. However, because of the inability to accept science *and* still retain faith, most of the modern world has abandoned the latter. It has been easy to create a seeming dichotomy between objective truth and subjective truth, and so we just relegated subjective truth to the dust heap of superstition, myth and unstable emotion. The modern sophisticated man has left anything and everything subjective behind, and now tries—or at least thinks he does—to work entirely in the objective realm. Strangely enough, he fails to grasp that he deals with much of the subjective in his daily life—his relationships with others for instance. Humans think all knowledge must be obtained by measurable and finite means, and it must be disseminated the same way. This is true for the man who enrolls in an institution of higher learning as well as the Internet wanderer engaged with Google and YouTube. We have managed to tangle up knowledge, wisdom, science and random facts into a rather wonderful Gordian knot that is impossible for the man without faith to untangle.

On a related educational note, (for that patient of yours who just registered for class) we have had a great hold on institutional education for some time now, and have spent years in developing theories, modules and statistics. We advance our ideas in traditional disciplines such as Economics, and come up with new ones, such as Sustainability, all the while generating a more costly endeavor. Soon, schools will be seen as simply another business that needs to make a profit, and it will be administered within such parameters by those with a very narrow focus. We have created a vast structure of organized, institutional educational platforms, which now concentrate almost entirely on preparing people to obtain employment and have completely abandoned the idea of educating individuals. In fact, few people can even agree on what an educated individual is supposed to know!

The sequential march of activity is promulgated with the eventual lucrative employment as the end goal. First, create a program of study designed for speed, then take the required classes, doing whatever is obligatory for the requisite grade, get the vital diploma and you are out the door! The whole endeavor has been turned into a factory, churning out graduates like so many GM cars, with only slight variations in the model. Though what happens afterwards—when the former students (trying all the while to achieve financial success) must navigate through life without the slightest experience in critical thinking or the remotest idea of wisdom—is another thing altogether. So with your patients, promote the fast-track diploma idea. Let them think that if they just get a degree—the rest of their life will be smooth sailing. Keep any old-fashioned notions of "knowledge" away from them… it should not be difficult at this point, as most colleges and universities have lost all trace of it.

Even more amusing has been our recent entrepreneurial companies, whose purported aim is to "help" students study, but *really* just exist to profit from student's disinclination to attend class. Thanks to these companies, one can, with their help, simply buy the lecture notes from another student. There are even businesses offering to take your online class for a fee, promising at the very least a B! As I mentioned above, we promote the adoption of dozens of new areas of study and delete time-honored ones that now seem outdated—history and languages for example. We have also made the "idea" of this education an inherent right rather than a privilege that is earned.

Again, remember the sticky adjacent strands of the spider's web. The subsequent mounting debt for education is a happy secondary consequence. All too soon, we will have an entire generation struggling under such a load of debt that they will eventually smother. In times past this path to a career was limited to doctors and attorneys who eventually had an income adequate to pay off the burden. Now we are enjoying seeing business and education majors think nothing of seeking loan after loan—all very comfortably justified in the name of education.

Additionally, we have promoted the concept of campus life. The university *provides* the life. First it was the sorority, then the campus food court and a place to hang out. Soon, we made necessities out of the student gym, counseling services, art/entertainment, health centers, attorney consultation, and the list goes on and on. Thus, higher education moves its focus (and budget) away from educating people to providing them with all they need in life. Rather than relying on their own selves for these services, they are now expected to be an inherent part of the educational package. Hence, the long drawn out years spent at various educational institutions are spent quite comfortably. We have students who have taken nearly a decade to get an undergraduate degree, all the while racking up more and more debt.

The atmosphere on college campuses has changed as well; we have created some tight knots there too. What used to be hallowed halls that venerated the accumulated wisdom of the past are now high-tech rooms rife with corruption and overpaid administrators constantly seeking additional revenue, and tenured faculty more intent on their present research (and remuneration) than quality teaching. Thanks to contemporary ideology (generated by us), learning is no longer reverenced. We are adroit at promoting comfort, contentment and self-worth, and enable students to pressure professors and administrators to change programs of study, dismiss invited speakers and disband organizations—all in the name of personal offense and inclusion.

Higher education is no longer a place where questioning students come to seek knowledge. (Unless it is whether extra credit is available...) It is instead a place for strident voices to be heard and personal opinion to be privileged. Students now demand to dictate content, curriculum and policy. We have dismissed any notion of learning from those who have spent years in active research (though of course we have had a negative hand in that pie as well), instead, social causes and personal affronts are to be applied to decision-making and what ought to pass as viable subject matter and methodology.

Use intellectual apathy and laziness to good effect here. Create a critical view in the minds of students of how much work they are expected to do, and how much of the curriculum is concerned with subjects they are not interested in, then nudge them on to protest these conditions as unfair and exclusionary. Shakespeare is well on his way to becoming obsolete!

Our personally-trained school administrators look at success in terms of numbers: how much tuition money they have coming in, how many new students are added each year, how many diplomas they turn out—it is all processed. So then, because of the dulling of the intellect caused by the addiction to entertainment (by the way, keep pushing that—see previous e-mails Homage to Hollywood and the Dull Edge of the Blade), we have a steeply declining retention rate and a sharply rising failure rate. Don't worry about the whole conspiracy unraveling as the administrators are inclined to put the blame on the faculty or suggest some new support program or training to solve the problem. We have created a generation that cannot even attend class regularly, let alone pay attention and engage in critical thinking. The requisite work to learn is a price so many students are unwilling to pay. They can't seem to connect the dots and so—for the most part—they don't try. It is an entitled generation and they believe they are entitled to an easy education—the most for their money with the least amount of work. Rather than cutting the Gordian knot like Alexander, they will just add to it.

Best,

Wormwood

Everything Is a Best Buy

My Dear Tempters,

This month in particular, you should be focusing on consumer indulgence. Oh, don't worry—we don't stress too much when they start their "Reason for the Season" posts and posits—for we know the dominant factor in the season *will be* buying and selling. Our "Reason for the Season" is to generate the *want* to prevail over the *need*. This is true all year round of course; we tend to have more success during the season of 'giving.'"

Humans are binary creatures. They are composed of spirit and a physical body—the two together constitute the soul of man. The Enemy wants them to have a mortal experience (we are not completely sure why this is) but he wants their spiritual self to have *at least* as much *if not more* force in their daily life as their physical self. (We are still at work attempting to get an assessment as to his expectations on this.) He wants them neither to ignore the body—so the medieval monk who we persuaded to live his isolated ascetic life obviously missed the point—nor have the body completely govern their life as so many of today's voluptuaries do. Apparently, they are to learn to fully and completely integrate the two. This binary nature is at once our great advantage, and also disadvantage, for when we can persuade humans to focus entirely on their physical self, they will forget, or at least neglect the spiritual. However, when the Enemy teaches their spirit (in league with *his* I might add, which is so grossly unfair!) to be strong enough to subsume the physical—then our cause is in danger. The more we emphasize the physical, the more we can draw them away from the spiritual. Apparently, the physical self becomes less dominant when the spirit self is ascendant. Since *we* do not have bodies—we cannot fully appreciate the state. What we do know from empirical studies is how successful we can be in emphasizing the worship of the body itself. So a parallel concentration here is the physicality of humans; their surroundings (i.e., home, car, clothes, etc.) that leads us to the great notion of *possessions!*

The list of real physical needs of human beings is quite a small one. Food, shelter, clothing and the means to provide these—that is about it. We have been able to extend this list far beyond what is reasonable. What I find so interesting in this endeavor is how we have managed to alter not only living habits and behaviors but thoughts and language as well. For example: the word *want* in generations past was typically used to describe something essential. One example—I regret having to draw upon—is its use in that vile but favorite story of Ebenezer Scrooge (oh, how we wish they would stop republishing that again and again!). The men who come asking Scrooge for donations say: "*We choose this time, because it is a time, of all others, when Want is keenly felt, and Abundance rejoices.*"* Here, the word *want* represents basic human needs (listed above) and what is suggested by this dreadful author is that the abundance of others can supply those needs. What we have been able to do today is alter the very meaning of *want*. "Wants" (notice the plural) are now things they have a strong desire to have but are not necessities. We capitalize on that type of desire and make it increasingly more difficult for humans to distinguish between *wants* and *needs*. It is most interesting that we can cause a complete reversal in the meaning of actions, words and concepts. We quite literally have the power to make black appear white!

Your job is to encourage buying, collecting, getting, having, owning, keeping and hoarding. Acquiring possessions should completely dominate their time and eventually so much of their space that they must buy a larger house and/or rent a storage facility just to make room for it all. They will work five days a week so they can spend the weekend buying. And lucky for us—now that so much purchasing is done online and delivered to their door, they don't even

---

*Charles Dickens, *A Christmas Carol*, (New York, 2013), 18.

have to get dressed and go out, but they are *still* focused on material goods—the physical world. There is no time for their spirit, because after buying, the residue of their time is usually spent on entertainment! (See Homage to Hollywood e-mail).

The commercial world is a great friend to us. We have manufacturers so completely worshipping the god of "profit" they will do almost anything to promote their wares. They easily persuade the unwary shopper into buying much more than planned for they make them believe they are getting a "deal." Never mind that they don't really need four packages of bows or six boxes of cards this Christmas, the "buy two, get one half off" has made the decision for them. Never mind that when Christmas is over they do not need more decorations and will not have space to store them, the "After Christmas Sale" is enough to persuade them to spend more the very next day. More is always *more* in the material world. More is always better. More is always out there waiting to be brought home. More is always on the verge of being unavailable if one doesn't hurry and get it. Sales can attract customers who were not initially in that particular market and send them home with the smug satisfaction of saving a dollar. Look what we have done with this seasonal business: the whole institution of Black Friday and Cyber Monday have been built on the notion of getting a good deal. They are actual named days on the calendar now!

Keep up your work with the manufacturers and designers—keep introducing new products—especially new products with a higher price tag. Your patients will then always have another new thing on their "want" list. Keep working with advertising; remember to alter appearances so they bear no resemblance to reality—you know what I mean—those home magazines showing the family dog sitting on the white sofa, or the cover girl faces with flawless skin. From Burger King to Banana Republic, you *must* make them turn the wants into needs so the "wants" should be appealing—the nicer car, the bigger boat, the more fashionable clothes, the larger home in the better part of town. You might think that these tactics work only on the wealthy, but they are just as effective with the lower economic classes because the important thing is to *spend*. It makes no difference if the spending is at Restoration Hardware or the local Dollar Store. The essential point is the patient's desire to acquire material goods. The lower income patient has the same problem as the high-end buyer—it is the single-minded focus and desire for the things of the world—things they almost never *really* need, things that are superfluous to their life, things that once bought become a burden rather than a blessing. The $15,000 designer couch and the ten-color eye shadow for $3, serve the same purpose for us. Though I do have to admit that our efforts at conniving humans into thinking something like, "This Gucci purse was on sale for only $300—it was *such* a good deal," brings so much glee into our sometimes dreary work that our toil is worth it in the end. If we can get them to waste and wear out their lives working for the sake of buying—we will have done our jobs well.

Best,
Wormwood

Go and Worry about Sin No More

Dear Tempters,

I have recently heard reports that some of you are slacking in your attention and allowing the Enemy's word to get to your patients. You simply cannot allow sincere pondering. In other words, don't leave them alone; if they insist on his words, you must dish it out to them personally. As I pointed out in an earlier e-mail, one of our techniques is using the Enemy's most well-known maxims for our own benefit. For example, one of these is: *loving one another as he loved them.* I know I have discussed this subject before, but it is vital that you understand how to twist his words.

Rather than searching through the New Testament and learning exactly how it was that he loved them, most humans just lump the whole idea of the Enemy's love as being broad and comprehensive and unending. Try to get your patients to regard that love of which he speaks as an open-armed, unconditional love that makes no reference to choice. Point them to the woman taken in adultery story (this is our best example, though it is ironically the Enemy's as well so don't let them read too closely).* In this instance, the leaders—who we had firmly in our control—were hoping he would say she had to be stoned according to the law. Instead, he condemned their own hypocrisy by telling them that whoever among them was without sin could cast the first stone. What is important for us is the next part. After they left, Jesus told the woman that he did not condemn her

---

*John 8:3-11

either. That is what our Comfortable Christians will focus on. He did *not* condemn the adulterous woman, thus follows in their minds the attendant, though unstated, conclusion that she is loved by him and so adultery is:

1. Not so bad
   Or
2. Easily forgiven.

What they do not like to apply to their life is the gritty reality of the rest of what he said, "Go, and sin no more." Thankfully for us, the New Testament account is silent on the woman's subsequent life. Oh, don't mention Magdalene—can't you amateurs distinguish between facts and our additive materials? We have mixed up all the Marys and unnamed women to such a degree that nothing can be seen with clarity—at least in the extant texts. This particular woman left the presence of the Enemy with a very different heart and she *did* come back to him, though the road was not an easy one. I personally had this information from Toadflax who was assigned to her, and who was subsequently demoted, I might add. When humans are reading these verses or religious teachers are teaching them, we try to have them promote the first line Jesus says and not the second. We want to remove any emphasis on sin and specific behavior, and instead concentrate on his great love. Since we have not been able to remove, alter or damage his love, and it is not only *real* but also *constant*—we have decided to manipulate it for our own ends. Thanks to Jesus declaring his love for humans— we can use his own words in our work.

His oft-repeated invitation, *"Come, unto me"* was uttered by him to all, without regard to past life mistakes, present uneasiness, or feeling of unworthiness. It was uttered to the despairing, the distracted, the disdainful and the disheartened—it is *still* being uttered by him in a thousand different voices in myriads of ways. Our success lies in the almost imperceptible alteration to each human of what it means to "Come unto [him]." We used to spend much time and effort with the *"I am unworthy"* approach. That was successful for ages as people just stayed away, wallowing in shame and rarely questioned why the Savior would have issued the invitation if he did not mean to have anyone actually respond.

Then we moved on to the *"I will first try to become worthy"* approach. This was pleasant to watch as they tried so hard to make themselves "good enough" to come to their Savior—they never quite grasped what *good enough* actually was, or comprehended the ultimate impossibility. So they got discouraged trying, and most gave up. They failed to understand the order of the process you see. They were always waiting *until* they felt good enough to come to him. The basic misunderstanding was that they thought you had to achieve a certain level of goodness *in order* to come—and what he wanted was for them to *just come* and then… we struggle putting this into words so I will not elaborate and really, we are as yet unclear just what the next step is anyway—it has something to do with the heart.

This scheme of getting them to try and work their way *to* him seems to have lost its broad appeal in recent years so we have lately worked—among believers, mind you—in a new direction. It goes like this: You are already there! He loves you, he loves everyone, he loves you unconditionally no matter what you have done or are doing or intended to do. He loves you and is waiting with open arms for you. Now that last part is *actually true* for the Enemy doesn't want them to wait until they feel ready or worthy or have climbed up on their own. It is this very aspect we work with, though we present it with a twist. Make them see that he alone will fix it (whatever *it* is); in fact, he *already has* so nothing is needed from them. We persuade humans that in his arms, they will not only feel loved but also justified, validated, authenticated, and confirmed in all they have built themselves up to be—it is their story after all! Then they can let everyone know that they live their daily life *in that state* and no longer need concern themselves with religious rules and unnecessary laws. All of that was an old-fashioned and unenlightened view of redemption anyway. If one had to *do* anything, their argument goes, it denies what Jesus has done. *Saved* is the salient word here.

I trust you see where I am going with this. The phrase, *"Come unto me"* does not just describe proximity in a physical or even spiritual sense. If these humans were wise enough to put all the scriptural pieces together, they would see the big picture. The Enemy's idea of someone "coming" to his son means to fall down at his feet in humble repentance, with a broken heart and a contrite spirit—it means change, everlasting change. It means giving up yourself—*all* of yourself and keeping nothing back. It means being willing not only to go where the Enemy wants him to go, but *be* what the Enemy wants him to be. It truly *is* a "come as you are" party, but it was never intended to be a "stay as you are" event. It is an all-or-nothing invitation (and most humans, if they ever realize that, will decline). That is why the description of his yoke and his burden can be *easy and light*—he makes it so. But the humans are to be *harnessed* into his yoke. They aren't coming to him to be congratulated, given a vacation, or to have a good time—a harness is for *work*. And they forget it is *his* harness—not one of their own making that fits loosely and doesn't rub, that one can slip in and out of at a moment's notice.

So, when we try to get our self-satisfied, entertainment-addicted, opiate masses moving where we want them, they must turn this generous but demanding invitation into a misunderstanding. To them it must just be an expression of his desire for their closeness and they turn that into his approval. He loves them, so surely he understands them, and so he calls to them on whatever terms it pleases them to come. By the way, while they are thinking of this, don't let them near the parable about the guest without the wedding garment. We have the whole process well transformed by now. What *we* describe in our whispers is "coming to him" without actually "coming to him," because the whole meaning of "coming" *is* change. He represents change, welcomes, encourages, nurtures, tutors, helps, demands, expects and facilitates change. That is what coming to him essentially means. In fact, we suspect, though nobody here is certain, what he has in mind is a *new* person entirely. We, on the other hand, encourage contentedness and complacency, indolence and indulgence, excuses and rationalizations. We help them think they have "come to him" without moving an inch!

Do you see the genius of our approach as they contemplate the Enemy? He really does emphasize his love for mankind, he really does forgive, and he wants humans to love and forgive one another. All we need to do here is have them spotlight small bits of his teachings rather than the whole. What we do *not* want is the part of his word that emphasizes change, the difficult parts. That we avoid at all costs. Try to create in your patient an aversion to the word *repentance* itself. Give him a medieval torture chamber feel for it. Tell him over and over that Jesus loves him just as he is. The truth of that will stick—for it *is* true, as we very well know—it is just *not* all. Avoid those in the Enemy's camp who have grasped the truth that his love also includes *his will* for them and that means change. Make their voices sound intolerant, narrow-minded and self-righteous.

The help we can expect from contemporary society is unprecedented. For we work in a society that is completely and contently self-absorbed and to have some opprobrious religious fanatic telling them to repent is not a welcome message. If someone brings the historical Jesus into the dialogue, we now have instituted very glib and quite sophisticated arguments to throw back at them. For those happy people who are content and consider themselves believers, they now have a customized God, and those religious radicals just don't understand that Christ died for all—no matter who they are and what they do!

Now, forget the New Testament and get your patients back to facials and football games, please!

Best,
Wormwood

MERRY MODERN CHRISTIANITY

My Dear Tempters,

I know all of you are concerned about your patient's belief in the Enemy. You have observed that nastily inherent propensity in humans. As one of his followers put it, *humans don't believe in God because they have proved he exists, rather they try endlessly to prove he exists because they can't help believing in him. He has established that in their hearts.*[*] Do not despair. In this scientific, pseudo-intellectual and so-called modern age, we have a great advantage over earlier periods. For, while *we* know that the Enemy is real, many humans think his existence has to be proven or revealed with a rational, scientific methodology. Thus, we are very successful in keeping the whole idea of a Supreme Being appearing as a ridiculous, old-fashioned notion that men in less sophisticated eras merely imagined to pacify their fears and cope with uncertainty. We persuade man that religion is a completely artificial construct. Here, the modern man (under our influence) will delve into past civilizations for his arguments and demonstrate how early man developed religious beliefs and practices.

We were hard at work even in those days, helping to create a pantheon of gods that were feared and needed constant propitiation by strange acts. Even after the real Enemy appeared on earth and that despised group of early followers changed the world, we were effectively working. Because of the lack of real, measureable (i.e., archaeological) evidence and the slow and complicated canonization

---

[*] Hugh B. Brown, *God is the Gardener*, BYU Commencement Speech, May 31, 1968.

of scripture, together with linguistically-based disbelief of prophetic authorship, we can easily persuade the skeptic that Christianity is just another in a long line of myths about gods coming to earth and the requisite homage of humans. Most people do not realize the myth can be a myth, and can also be real. Beginning in the nineteenth century, a large number of erudite scholars effectively diminished belief in a *real* Son of God, demonstrating that there were no actual miracles, or a resurrection from the dead but rather wishful thinking and artful deception. Thus, Christians join the Egyptians, Sumerians, Greeks, Hindus and any number of other ancient people who practiced man-made religion.

Textual criticism of the bible has been an enormous help in this department. The nineteenth century was one of our great periods where so many keenly intellectual individuals—many of them former believers—became influential on our side as they realized that there were variations in the early manuscript versions of the epistles of Paul, or some other such elusive and inconsequential philological details. True it is that the Bible took a while to be gathered into its present canon, and true it is that there are problems in its compilation, but the whole point of the scriptural record— which these critics missed entirely—was its function in revealing the Enemy to them. The problems they found (and believe me it was easy to generate them) including deliberate omissions, careless scribes, and even outright interference in the transmission process, really have not affected that main function—much to our chagrin! Thankfully, many throw the Enemy himself out with the texts and dismiss it all as unscientific, unverifiable, contradictory and imaginative.

One of the things atheists love to do is publish scathingly superior commentaries about the ignorant deluded Christians who don't even realize that even their beloved holidays were built on the detritus of pagan festivals—the poor dupes! (The Atheists I mean, not the Christians.) They miss the point entirely, which is just what we want. Today, we have books and blogs and an endless array of Internet sites that we hope the innocent believer can read with growing horror as they finally *find out* the "truth." Many whose faith has been shaken by clever arguments will be easily lured with the attendant idea that they can now be liberated from the arbitrary constraints formal religion imposes on them. For why (we have them ask) continue to uphold religious standards that prevent their living a full and free life, when faith is no longer a living thing? Thanks to the many distractions and preoccupations of the modern world, it is easy for believers to lose the faith they may have absorbed as a child—the faith of their parents and grandparents. They needn't become hardened atheists themselves, for indifferent agnostics or lazy disciples will do just as well. The delightful irony is that they think they are shedding the fetters of old-fashioned morality and convention when they leave religion behind, little realizing they are stepping straight into our ever-tightening but unseen chains.

Another aspect that has furthered our cause is the shortcomings—if not downright malicious behavior—of those who espouse Christianity. Humans rarely miss the chance to hold up one bad example as representative of the whole. So, all we needed was an immoral priest, a lying bishop, or a money-loving preacher, and once again the whole is dismissed as being false. Humans like to label and stereotype (thanks to us), and that particular inclination has generated a negative approach to the historicity of the church since the Enemy's appearance on the scene.

We are also *very* happy with the intellectual conclusion that Jesus was a great moral teacher. There is no harm in that for our side; in fact, it is pure genius. Great moral teachers can be admired. One does not need to *do* anything they say, just admire what is said from a distance. Additionally, Jesus as a great moral teacher does not stand out in any distinct way from other great moral teachers of the past. His gift then is not one of salvation but merely of philosophizing. As long as Jesus is just a man, no matter how impressive, our cause is quite safe. It is when they accept him as a God who can at once redeem, heal, and have compassion on the human state—that is when they move dangerously beyond our amendment. Your task then is to keep them admiring the historical Jesus (*if* such a person *even* existed, I mean really—can they prove it?), and have them focus their attention on their immediate needs and surroundings and busyness of life. Jesus's teachings will then be in the same comfortable category as Aristotle's or Buddha's or Emerson's—something quaint and faintly profound that one can paraphrase and post on a Facebook page within a decorative border.

Best,
Wormwood

Hello, Noise, My Old Friend

My Dear Tempters,

I want to discuss one of our tactics that has so much potential today—it is the advantage we can make of noise. If we could measure the world's collective noise from any five-minute period today and compare it to a five-minute period a hundred years ago, the difference would be astonishing. The world is a noisier place now. What is enlightening though, for our work, is to measure the noise made by or listened to just one individual within a twenty-four-hour period. When you compare that with a similar individual even fifteen years ago, well, let me just say we can celebrate our success! These are our halcyon days. Noise on the whole; traffic, business, construction, dogs, airplanes and the rest is helpful to us in creating the cacophonic environment in which we flourish. However, as I have told you before, our best efforts are with the individual patient, and here, the noise level and its constancy is *most* effectual.

In order to grasp the essentials, you need to understand something about the Enemy. To the best of our knowledge, he works most efficiently and effectively in the still moments. Oh, I know that he has had some very devout servants who were great orators and powerful songs that touch souls, but eventually, it all boils down to the Enemy working in the heart of one person. That kind of work (we do not actually comprehend the conditions or exact processes at this point) needs a quiet environment. This we certainly *do* know for a fact. So, our business is to keep quiet and *especially* complete silence far from our patients. Now, we do a good job with the sounds of the city or even annoying crickets chirping in the country, but we have needed to do much more on an individual basis, and since we can harness all sorts of technology in our behalf—Presto! Enter the personal music list.

This began in the '50s with transistor radios and the record player. We eventually moved on to 8-tracks, cassette tapes, and finally CDs. Now we have broken all barriers with mp3 players, iPods, the Cloud, Bluetooth, etc., all with lovely ear plugs (buds—they call them.). What we have created here is the ability (and desire) of humans to have something "playing" in their ear every available moment: in the car, in the office, while jogging, at school, studying, eating, and shopping. It becomes an addiction. They cannot function without some kind of sound on. Of course, *what* they are listening to is another avenue of attack I have addressed before and will again. The point is they *need* their music; they pride themselves on the number of songs they have downloaded and know exactly how much memory they need for more. This becomes an identifying aspect of their very character. (Get them to judge one another based on music preferences, by the way).

Commercial establishments also contribute to our efforts with their sound systems, which, at the present, even move far beyond their confines and blare out into the parking lot. You cannot find a bank, doctor, store, or even a gas station that doesn't have some background music. This sound—ranging from the soothing (what they used to call "elevator music") to the loud and jarring—is what I call "technology noise." Using technology noise is one of our most effective weapons against what the Enemy calls his "Spirit." More than anything else, that revolting power of his *must* be kept away from our patients! Technology noise will block the spirit. Trust me, we have tested this out in a multitude of cases in varying circumstances, and it is a proven method of resistance.

We have been able to foster the love/need for sound to the extent that there is now an actual abhorrence, I might even say fear, of silence. Notice how many homes have the TV on even when no one is actually sitting down and watching it. They have it on so much that it becomes part of the environment—like the air they breathe—and they *keep* it on. This does marvelous things to relationships and communication because people cannot focus on more than one thing at a time, so the distraction of the TV affects real, deep, meaningful interaction. But more importantly, the dependence on and being accustomed to sound/noise makes it almost impossible for a person to stop and think deeply. They just cannot get past the silence. Instead of rejoicing in the moment—such as when they are praying for example—they want to hurry to get on with their day or hurry and jump into bed. In fact, some humans even need a machine that creates the sound of rain, or the ocean, or even static noise in order to sleep! Thus, many of our patients can be led through a whole day and not have had even a pause in the noise—let alone anything close to what one would call some quiet time. They have become uncomfortable with quiet and so too with any attendant thoughtfulness—the kind that comes when the mind and heart unite in pondering. If you remember what I discussed in my Hollywood e-mail about the constancy of entertainment, you will see how that weapon is used in conjunction with this fight against quiet. The dependence on the first (entertainment) will eventually cancel out the desire for the second (quiet).

Noise is also very helpful as we try to engender contention and misunderstanding between humans. Real communication with each other requires the words to be heard clearly and the ideal condition for that is quiet—without any distraction. If we can keep the Bluetooth on and the volume up in the car when couples are driving somewhere, then the likelihood of effectual communication is lessened. The inability to listen closely and hear clearly is of course the obvious reason but another advantage you have is that one of them might be distracted by a favorite song or a catchy new tune or even an interesting NPR report and only half listen to their companion. Hopefully, the lack of communication can then be galvanized into real problems. Same thing at home: keeping the music or TV on and the volume up will provide a nice distraction and distance between family members or visitors, and diminish the value of any conversation that takes place.

One of the patterns we have observed in the Enemy's devoted disciples (those whom we consider the *most* difficult patients) is that they spend a good part of their day in silence. It appears as if they are listening (to what though?). This behavior—as one would expect—most often accompanies prayer and reading of the scriptures. However, this is not exclusively so, for very often, just at random points throughout their day—walking, sitting in their offices or living room, or driving in a car—they have apparently *chosen* quiet rather than select from our vast offering of technology noise. This fact needs to be understood, for the random noises of the world like the sounds of children playing or a car horn, are not what distracts humans from feeling the Enemy—our technology noise, however, does!

So your job is to keep your patient away from silence, away from the quiet moments when he begins to sink deep inside himself. When he moves in that direction, put a little tune in his head, his favorite—or even one he hates. Flash an image of a movie with a particularly intense sound track. Remind him he was going to change his ring tone. Prompt him to pick up where he left off on that rather loud game he was playing last night—*anything* to get the noise back on. Noise is our dearest friend.

Best,
Wormwood

Go to Extremes!

My Dear Tempters,

I hope that you are gleaning certain principles from my counsel to you in these e-mails. One you should have observed is the very great benefit our cause receives from extremes in thought and behavior. For us, the far end of the spectrum on any given subject is the most fruitful. Now, this may seem at odds with the Enemy's plan, for he wants their complete and total allegiance, which certainly sounds extreme to us. However, that kind of complete giving up of their "self" is not what I mean when I say extreme behavior. In that case, it is not extreme because it is given over to the Enemy. What I have in mind is the single-minded, lopsided, overloaded, tunnel-vision focus on one aspect of their life. The reason this works well with our agenda is that, it is effective with the positive, as well as the more obvious negative. When humans fail to apply moderation to any part of their daily life, the scales tip and they are out of balance. Diet, exercise, learning, work, child-rearing, almsgiving, politics, patriotism, pacifism, recreation, money, social causes, discouragement, worry, anxiety, anger, paranoia, injustice, fear, even a particular gospel "hobby-horse"—almost anything can go on this list.

If we can nudge them into a mental preoccupation and an obsessive zeal for one thing, they are much easier to lead into warped ideas and false assumptions. They begin to view the world through the lens of their fanaticism and it turns into a kind of mental and emotional anorexia as they cease to see things as they really are. This can evolve into all kinds of lovely problems with their families and associates as the patient begins to develop animosity for everyone who does not agree with or understand them. An intellectual can be made to feel he is so far above others who do not have advanced degrees that they are scarcely worth talking to. A human rights activist can be made to lose patience with anyone who will not join his cause. A health advocate can look down on the masses that consume Pepsi and pastries. I trust you see the picture?

Now, my focus here is how this principle of extremes can be used in certain instances on the inner workings of moods and emotions. When your patients begin thought processes in a certain area, you can quickly move them through a series of ideas and images, all the while manipulating other conditions (like fatigue or a sore back) to affect a nicely negative end result. You must exploit the human propensity to self-denigration. Oh, there might be a certain amount of what you would call "healthy" self-assessment out there, where humans see what is lacking and make attempts to improve—that kind of thing we will routinely fight against. What I am referring to is that woebegone, lowly opinion of their worth and the failure to see any value in what they do. It is easy to push that descent into discouragement and then commence pulling them down another step, and then another.

Take a busy mother for example: she tries her best to teach her children good habits and correct principles. The fruits of that teaching are usually long in ripening. All she sees is the cluttered house and the constant bickering, and she has likely lost her temper more than once that day. She goes to bed quite convinced that she is not only a lousy mother but also a quite ineffectual one. Here is where you jump in to push the extreme. Don't let her drift off to sleep without getting in some good digs about her appearance—after all, she has really let herself go lately!

Add in some stabs about her lack of a college degree and neglect of talents she may have had in former years. Remind her of the tight financial situation they are in with her sloppy budget attempts, the worn furniture, and you will have helped her to a nice slow descent into depression. Don't forget to have her think of several friends that appear to be much more "with it" so she can fall short by comparison. Humans will always compare their worst with the best of others. Women's expectations for themselves are generally high, and so they are especially prone to the feeling of forever falling short. Thus, when you point out the many areas of failure you can be assured she will fall for it. Hopefully, she will wake up the next morning completely discouraged and with an overwhelming desire just to stay in bed.

You see how this works? You apply my earlier comments about extremes. Feelings of discouragement are part of a mortal life, but pushing them to the extreme creates depression. That is what we want you to do—push. Humans are their own worst enemies (far more than we are) because they are the harshest of critics and judges. Add a long list of failures and fiascos to the start of any reflective moment. There will always be times when humans have under-performed and they feel the effects of self-administered criticism. In itself, that is productive for them. Our work is to turn the process into a massive attack on every facet of their life. This piling on of one negative thought after another is not limited to the sleep-deprived overwhelmed mother. It can be just as effective on the busy insurance salesman. Tell him because that particular sales pitch did not go well he really doesn't have much skill. Perhaps his grades in school were not the best—bring that up. Tell him he can never work hard enough; others will inevitably be more successful. Remind him of the heavy mortgage, the noisy children and needy wife waiting at home after a particularly difficult day, and you will have him!

On the flip side, what is actually preferable because it centers on pride, is the other kind of behavior humans are also prone to—that of thinking well of themselves. You know what I mean, the "power of positive-thinking" approach. By all means, push that to the extreme. Your patient might be pretty optimistic to begin with. That is where you commence your attack. A slight whisper that they have done so well they should be commended—and they will soon be commending themselves. Start a list of virtues and accomplishments in their head, and here again, don't forget to use comparisons. In this instance, suggest how much better they appear in the spotlight than those around them. It works with the affluent achievers as well as Joe six-pack. This extreme will lead not only to pride but to certain levels of complacency and of course, the subsequent judgment of others, as noted earlier.

Lull them into an "*all is well*" mode. This extreme approach is especially applicable to the over-achievers. You can get fathers to neglect their wives and children under the guise of achieving financial success. Help him feel driven to take on one more task or spend just a few more hours in pursuit of his goals. You can motivate ambitious women to let nothing get in the way of their move up the career ladder, certainly not their spouse or children. Others can be persuaded to volunteer for so many causes they work themselves into exhaustion.

When you have moved your patient to the extreme edge, what you will want to watch for and avoid at all costs—is any movement toward the Enemy for help. This is vital for both your negative work (depression) and your positive (pride), for the Enemy poses a danger to your best efforts on either side. Remind the "negatives" that they are so far gone; they are past the point of any improvement. We often have them buried in such a heavy cloud of guilt and despair that exertion is almost impossible, so it should not be difficult. Repeat to your "positives" that they don't actually need him, they are less inclined to feel the need for help anyway, so that should not be difficult. Encourage the complacent self-approval they have fostered while still keeping the "better than others" arrogance. But above all—push the extremes!

Best,
Wormwood

THE GOD OF THE GYM

My Dear Tempters,

I often hear reports that tempters are concerned when their patient has taken a gym membership, believing that their improved health will affect their efforts to turn them to gluttony and dissipation. This just shows the younger generation's ignorance about temptation. You have a golden opportunity here. Yes, it is true that as the body and the soul are closely intertwined (something we in our state cannot really comprehend) and when one is experiencing optimal health he might be more inclined to spiritual activity. However, most humans do not have a concrete idea of this fact so you do not have cause to be concerned.

What you do not want to miss is the chance this gives you to turn his attention wholly to his body—not as a vehicle for his spirit—but as an object of worship in and of itself. Yes, you read that correctly—I really mean worship. You surely have seen what our minions have done in recent years? Cult temples in homage to the body everywhere, endless products on the market from high-tech treadmills to smoothie cook books, expensive running shoes, and whole lines of sports clothing endorsed by famous names. It is in essence a religion, and the cult gains in adherents every day. Money, time and attention are the votive offerings. Of course, humans rarely realize what has happened to them that, in fact, they have found a new deity. They begin going to the gym with the most simple and sincere intention of making their body stronger and getting healthy, and it is true that some of them can stick to just that motivation.

Moderation is never their strong point, however, and with the all too pervasive tendency toward comparison, they soon want to be "as strong as," or "as thin as..." someone else. Weight and size are only meaningful comparatively, for what is the ideal? It is something we on our side have imposed on society in these days, as we have in the past. So your patients will begin with health but soon, how good their body looks compared to everyone else, is what will go through their minds. Let him get the idea that if he could spend two hours a day instead of the one hour he has squeezed in out of the twenty-four, he too will be able to have a flat stomach and muscles like the man across the room, or she will soon have thin thighs and buff arms like the woman on the adjacent treadmill.

The gym is the ideal place for comparison. It is also the ideal place for the worship of the body. For men, this will give you the added advantage of giving them the chance to view the scantily-clothed bodies of females other than their wives. It is not his fault after all—I mean, where else can he look? Help him feel conscious, while his eyes wander, that he ought to be as young-looking and fit at forty-five as he was at twenty-five.

Humans wage a fierce fight against the aging process almost without our help. There must be something important the Enemy wants them to learn from aging—we are not sure as yet what that is—but we can easily turn this thought around when it flits in by reminding them of someone they know that *has* been able to have a twenty-five-year-old body at age forty-five. They are constantly bombarded by images (digitally altered, though their cognizance of that is minimal at best) that entice them to want to look younger. The imagery serves as another form of comparison.

Yes, I know the Enemy *has* given them dietary laws from time to time. Keep the focus there and it can be used as justification for enormous amounts of time spent on the body. They might begin with health but it will eventually lead to worship. Thankfully, we have made sure there are plenty of mirrors in most gyms. The dietary laws of the Enemy are, after all, more about obedience than health—but keep to a very narrow approach there.

We have been quite successful in this focus on the body, more so for women than men, I think. If you look at most women today, you will see what progress has been done. They too, start out thinking they need to eat healthy and are usually conscious that they need to lose weight. This is of course, when we are at our most effective—we are always "commencing with a truth"* and so they do not recognize the distortion into error by immoderation. So with diet and health, they are initially following good counsel and up-to-date scientific studies—always encourage that aspect.

Soon though, we turn them into fanatics, which transform this *one* part of their life into *the* most important part of their life, and their central focus each day. One of the most recent and quite successful branches of this compulsive behavior is the obsession with endurance training and competition. The idea of pushing their body to its limit and expanding those limits beyond all reason is a flourishing field for us. The body is going to break down eventually and many bodies come already broken. The great and central truth of the Enemy is the promise of a literal, bodily resurrection. They will all be made new (a horrible thought for us), and yet they train their body as if they can somehow make it new themselves.

There is almost as much obsession here as the ancient Egyptians had with their mummification! The hours spent in training for the myriads of triathlons and their derivatives alone are reason for us to rejoice. What better thing can we do than have them focus on their own body? What if that many hours were spent helping others instead? Or, in the development and training of their minds, or hearts? The Enemy, of course, encourages the notion that the mind is stronger than the body and one can endure more than one thinks, and so this whole idea of endurance might have its origin in truth—but it once again thanks to us—has gotten far beyond the Enemy's principles. For what is the purpose of it all? And we have the added advantage of capitalizing on man's natural competitive nature—they always want to be better than others. The whole idea of a race promotes competition and comparison. That is not what their darling Paul had in mind, by the way.

I get quite amused as they never wonder how this obsession of health can be at odds with something the Enemy said when he was

---

* Shakespeare, *Macbeth*, Act I.3.136.

here on earth, about it not being what man takes into his mouth that was important but what came out of his mouth—they simply do not see the connection. Of course, there will always be those wiser mortals who fully recognize the principle of moderation—they will be healthy but keep the whole process in perspective (and to themselves) those you usually cannot sway into excess. But for the many for whom you can influence, this obsessive tendency also has the frequently added pleasure of seeing them think less of their fellow creatures who do not have the discipline that they do.

Additionally, they can easily annoy everyone around them by harping on and on about their latest triumph. Here, technology comes back into play (see my previous e-mail) because we heartily encourage posting images and accounts of their fitness plan, healthy meals and latest endurance race. It starts off sincerely and humbly, but pride is soon blossoming to our delight. And if that doesn't happen, we can easily fall back into the opposite target—helping them think they never *will* compare and their bodies are beyond help. Soon you will have them feeling they cannot be happy while they are unhappy with their bodies. This is of course most effective with females, but even some males are prone to it. Foster in them a belief that their self-worth is at stake and you can see them slide into a depressive state that will glean great rewards, all the while paying for that expensive gym membership.

Best,
Wormwood

Souring the Uses of Adversity

My Dear Tempters,

Judging from your last e-mail, you are obviously not familiar with Shakespeare's line, "*Sweet are the uses of adversity*,"* as I can see that most of you are making a serious mistake in thinking that your patient's time of trouble is *your* easy time. I made the same mistake myself long ago. It appears reasonable to assume that problems, struggles, pain and miserable circumstances are the conditions in which we can just sit back in a comfortable chair and watch the fun. Misery is, after all, what we want for them.

When humans experience serious suffering, especially when they suffer through no fault of their own, the whole notion of the Enemy's omniscience and benevolence comes into question. His very existence is sometimes doubted. Junior tempters, at this juncture, think they can just move in with some clever little, sophisticated, negative whisperings and the game is theirs. Those of us who have worked and watched through the years know better. For, unfortunately, this is not always the case. It appears to be an unfathomable paradox to us (and to them) but during the worst and most difficult times, humans can truly come to know the Enemy. Our first intimation of this idea arose during the long ago episode in "the garden." We assumed the triumph to be all on our side when the consequence of that particular choice was enacted. However, the Enemy's reference to the ground being cursed *for thy sake* and the sorrow and sweat of the brow business caused some questions among us even then. We have come to realize the problem. We can use pain and suffering

---

*Shakespeare, *As You Like It*, Act II.1.12.

to our advantage, *but so can the Enemy!* It almost seems as if he had *planned* it that way.

Though humans may want to "Curse God and die,"* during these down times, what actually *can* happen is the annoying creatures turn from the everyday mundane and begin to focus on the absolutely essential. The Enemy has apparently ingrained within them just exactly *what* that essential is—*him!* That is *not* what we are working for! Remember all my other e-mails? We want distraction, preoccupation with "*me*," and distance from the Enemy. Adversity can make the fog and obscurity we generate fade away and produce some remarkably clear views into reality.

So what you need to do immediately when troubles raise their hydra-like heads is to push one of the following conclusions:

1. There is no God.
2. There is a God but he is unjust and cruel.

Either of these will serve our purpose. When humans suffer, or observe the general suffering in the world, they assume (with their limited understanding) that if God exists and he is good then he would prevent suffering. Hence, in their myopic view, God does not exist. They cannot see him. They cannot hear him. They cannot feel him *because* they are suffering and the world is suffering. Suffering to them is just more fuel for the fire of general unbelief. Keep them in that bitter and resentful state. It will lead to cynicism and pessimism, and eventually complete rejection of the divine.

Though I do have to add, in the extremities of suffering there *are* no real atheists. In certain circumstances, all humans will— unbidden, cry out to a power higher than themselves. They may not recognize or label this a prayer to the Enemy, but that essentially is what it is. We cannot absolutely wipe out all traces of that connection and inclination, much as we might try, even we admit this sad fact. A good strategy is to pile on to his specific pain and suffering, the pain and suffering of the larger world community. He will begin

---

*Job 2:19

with what he considers his own unfair anguish and then attach the sorrows he sees around him. This is particularly effective if you keep him to a global perspective. Bring to his mind the people in difficult circumstances on the other side of the world that he has read about in the news: from politics to hurricanes, and from child abuse to economic depression, there should be plenty to observe. These detached stories can add to his resentment without his being at all connected to anyone by a shared experience. Under no conditions allow him to form an association with someone who is next door (so to speak) for those individuals he *could* actually share sorrows with—and that is the last thing we want!

Humans who go through difficulties together tend to help one another by the sheer fact of fellowship. We have found that even the annoying neighbor will pitch in and help sandbag the house during a flood. Avoid that. Have him believe that nobody actually understands what he is going through. Help him compare his suffering with others and always conclude that his is the worst. Hopefully, his time of suffering will have the effect of turning him completely away from God and religion and his fellow creatures.

If God did exist, he would not allow the turmoil. Anger is a good tool to use here. In this frame of mind he will usually lash out at those trying to help and reject counsel, advice and support, blaming everyone and everything for his troubles. Loved ones, especially become targets during this period of misery, bringing additional mayhem for us to exploit. The Enemy hopes that adversities will soften hearts—we push for a hardened one. Keep the self-pity at a high level and prevent him from performing any kind of service to others—that is paramount to remember if you want the full effects of adversity.

You can also encourage an alternative human response to suffering. A sincere believer in God wonders why he suffers. He pleads for the trial to be taken away and it usually is not, at least not within his time frame. The heavens seem to be silent. During these periods, time moves agonizingly slow. If you can get him to concentrate on himself and his own suffering, he might not dismiss the notion of God altogether *but* he will conclude that God is indifferent to suffering. Or even better, suggest he take all things personally and conclude that he is unworthy of God's love and care. He is suffering because he deserves it. He is being punished. Now this might not be too difficult to suggest because a great deal of human suffering *does* follow the law of the harvest. They do bring on their own suffering, i.e., lung cancer from choosing to smoke for forty years, etc. Interestingly enough, you can often get *those* particular patients to blame everyone *except* themselves. But even if this is not the case, their own self-doubts and past mistakes can loom large during adversity and we can help construct all sorts of self-flagellating reasons for the pain.

What they usually fail to fathom—and this is where you must be careful—is that the Enemy apparently uses pain and suffering as a good teacher does a particularly difficult assignment. Students may curse the teachers during it, wish they had never taken the class, and feel like dropping out, but after the course has ended they realize how much they have learned. That is exactly what happens during human suffering *if* the creatures will allow it—they learn. They learn disgusting things like humility and then, much to our dismay, the Enemy becomes the center of the lesson. They come to know him through learning patience, long-suffering, fortitude, compassion for the suffering of others, the courage to go on in the face of pain, and so on and so forth ad nauseam.

Many of our great losses have occurred during adversity. There *are* sweet uses for it (damn Shakespeare anyway). That is why we do not necessarily rejoice when we see it happening with our patients. It is a risky and tricky maneuver to bring about the results that we want, rather than the Enemy's. He does not make the path smooth for them. It is instead narrow, rugged and uphill, but he is willing to risk our influence during those times because he knows the potential for growth. We, on the other hand, want to promote the broad path that is soft on their feet (see The Green Road for more on that).

One way we do this during adversity is to turn them to seek momentary relief from pain. The possibilities are many and very effectual: alcohol, drugs (even legitimate prescriptions can do the trick), pornography, or other forms of distractions. Instead of meeting their challenges head on, they will do their utmost to forget about them—even when they know it is only temporary. And then of course, the very form of their fleeting relief exacerbates the original adversity—exactly what we want—remember the sticky strands of the spider web.

Above all, keep them asking *why* rather than *what*. They get nowhere when they question why they suffer, but they will get very far (from us!) if they once begin to ask (the Enemy!) what he wants them to do. Suggest that if they knew why—they could overcome the adversity. The Enemy would rather they shed all the trappings of self-concern and humbly seek his will. Humility, real humility, is *always* inimical to our work. If they ever get to that point you have likely lost the game.

Best,
Wormwood

MIRROR, MIRROR

My Dear Tempters,

You will often find some clues to our strategy (and the Enemy's) in the myths and stories that have developed among humans because, though they are generally speaking dull-minded twits, they will occasionally figure out what we are about and create stories that illuminate our work. One of these which adults dismiss as merely a children's tale (and so have not learned from), is *Snow White and the Seven Dwarves*. We, however, refer to it as the Mirror Principle, and even though this particular story does not end well for our side, it is instructive nevertheless.

You will need to look up the story if you are unfamiliar with it (and there are various versions from the original Brothers Grimm), but the essentials for our discussion are these:

1. The queen was obsessed with viewing herself in the mirror.
2. The queen needed constant reassurance that not only was she beautiful but also the *most* beautiful.
3. Snow White never looked in the mirror, never thought about what she looked like or how she appeared to others but instead just helped and served (even those weirdo dwarves).
4. The queen is miserable—just where we want humans— and Snow White ends up happy ever after, just where we *do not* want humans.

So, the moral of the story as far as we are concerned, is: get humans to spend their time looking in the mirror. I have written on this subject before more than once—in the Battle of Self and Selfie-Esteem. I do so

87

again, at the risk of sounding like a broken record, because this is one of our strongest weapons in fighting the Enemy. *We advocate, endorse, push, promote, promulgate, prefer, present, sponsor, support, spread and shove mirrors!* Keep them looking into mirrors everywhere and all the time—both literally and figuratively. If we can get humans to look at themselves constantly, they will fail to look up and around them. That is, they will fail to look up to the Enemy, and around at their fellow sojourners on this earth. Hopefully, you have been reminded just now with that last sentence, of the Enemy's admonition about the two greatest commandments. The mirror keeps them preoccupied with self, and as far as we are concerned, that is the best state they can be in.

Now there are various ways you can utilize the Mirror Principle. You can push the world's idea of beauty and youth. Emphasize clothing and other personal adornment as much as possible. Notice there are plenty of mirrors in clothing stores. New styles, new brands, new fads, all of these begin and end with mirrors. Don't forget hair and nails! And, have you noticed that the application of women's make-up has now become an art form in itself, complete with YouTube video demonstrations—all quite unabashedly mirror-centered. The proliferation of products and suppliers catering to the Mirror Principle has reached an all-time high and we are quite justifiably proud.

We are also very effective in getting women to peer anxiously into the mirror every morning aghast at the encroaching lines and wrinkles they find. So then we send them out to purchase expensive products promising to eliminate the effects of age on their faces and bodies. And, no matter how little results they actually *see* after using it, they will continue to keep searching for some miracle cream that will make them young again. All of that has the effect of sending them *back* to the mirror to look for any progress. They will preen and pose and anguish about the size of their thighs—not to mention varicose veins. They will try various hairstyles and colors. They will make sure their teeth are not only straight but also brilliantly white.

The highpoint of all of this is that we can frequently move them on to more drastic measures that involve costly surgery. Do you see the brilliance of this focus? The Enemy wants them to look forward to what he promises as an eternal body, that whole "resurrection" thing he talks about. He doesn't want them to spend their time, attention and money on delaying the aging process or worrying about their weight, rather he wants them to hope for something infinitely better and more certain. He wants them to forget about themselves entirely. But because we have put this giant *mirror* in front of them, they cannot forget—they only see the mortal body here and now. They cannot look beyond and trust that he will really *"make all things new."* And believe me, the male sex is not immune to this idea either, though they will focus less on their gray hair and more on their muscle tone. Keep pushing the fitness thing there. (See The God of the Gym e-mail... remember I mentioned the number of mirrors in gyms.)

Additionally, you can help push a mental preoccupation with themselves and how they appear to others. In this avenue, you do not suggest the literal mirror as much as the figurative one. Your patient can be the kind of person who is unconcerned with looks but still very much concerned with themselves. How they *feel*, how they *used* to feel, how they *might* feel in the future, how they are *treated*, how they were *raised*, what phobias they have, how the world's conditions affect them, what they *need*, what they *want*, what they *have* or *do not have*—the list is endless. This sense of self is always the center of their life and *always will be* unless they willfully cast it aside. I say willfully *because* it is not a natural tendency to do so. Keep them away from individuals who are themselves in the middle of that "casting aside" process, and more especially those who have completely done so. They *do* exist, I assure you! What you want is for your patient to have a sense of self-consciousness *all the time,* so that they never quite let go of it.

The quest to "feel good" about themselves begins in front of the mirror. Humans will go to great lengths to obtain this elusive state of "feeling good about themselves." (See Selfie-Esteem on that futile endeavor). The point is to generate *all* their concentration on looking in the mirror. This kind of figurative mirror can be enlarged exponentially as they go about their daily life. Whether at work or school or home—all of their absorption is on themselves. This can lead to an endless supply of problems and complaints as they interact with others. It can also promote selfishness and discontent as they will never, *ever*, have enough attention or worldly goods, or easiness of life. They will never achieve a state of peace and equilibrium as long as they look inward. They will usually never reconcile their internal anxieties about the past or present or their concern for the future. In fact, the more they focus on themselves, the less they will "feel good." They cannot seem to remember the Enemy's words about "losing" themselves. Here again you can push it to the extreme of seeking counseling, and hopefully the attendant strong medication.

You can also promote the comparison game—that was the queen's obsession. Her beauty was not a satisfying entity in itself, only in terms of comparison. Pride is the frame of that particularly large mirror. In this state, humans *are* looking at their fellow creatures; however, it is only to compare and then either to criticize or to envy. They would not do either if not for so much daily "mirror" time. You can easily persuade them that they "look" either better or worse than others—it does not matter which of those two paths they go down as both lead to our camp.

I hope you all realize that the technology of the present day and the inundation of social media are just other forms of the Mirror Principle. Blogs, Facebook, Twitter, Instagram, Snapchat, and whatever else is now out there—I have a hard time keeping up as that is not my department down here; they are all centered in self-absorption. The Mirror Principle at work. Oh, I realize that there is a small percentage of the population who use technology sort of altruistically, but not the majority. These new devices are not much different from the wealthy matron in ancient Rome, looking into her bit of polished bronze or showing her neighbor her jewelry (remember the story of the woman who visited the mother of the Gracchi)?* We just keep updating the kinds of mirrors available.

Last but not least—while you are at work setting up your mirrors—keep the humans away from the Enemy's words as much as possible. His whole message is anti-mirror.

Best,
Wormwood

---

*Valerius Maximus, *Factorum ac dictorum memorabilium libri IX* (IV, 4, *incipit*).

The Drowsy Life and Smoldering Lamp

My Dear Tempters,

I take for the title of this e-mail, something that one of the Enemy's filthy servants wrote as a sort of preface for his discussion of certain parables given during that terrible time of the Incarnation. He was referring to the parables in Matthew 25, The Parable of the Ten Virgins, The Parable of the Talents, and the Parable of the Sheep and Goats. Stop rolling your eyes at my inclusion of the proper titles here! I told you we must be aware of what the Enemy taught in order to plan our counter-attack. Now back to my subject, this is what he (the servant) said:

"Therefore, to impress yet more indelibly upon their minds the lessons of watchfulness and faithfulness, and to warn them yet more emphatically against the peril of *the drowsy life and smoldering lamp*, He told them the exquisite parables…"[*]

My message today is to impress upon you—even *more* indelibly—that the drowsy life and smoldering lamp is *exactly* what we hope for you to achieve with your patients. This particular and insufferable servant had apparently identified our strategy quite accurately more than a hundred years ago. The Enemy reminded his followers to be "watchful." We try to get them to be complacent, contented, to put off any definite action until later, to enjoy the moment, to relax their defenses, to reduce their stress level and to be satisfied with their efforts. Then we talk them into considering themselves

---

[*] Frederic W. Farrar, *The Life of Christ*, (Portland, 1972), 545.

watchful. Most of the time they are not exactly sure what it is they are watching for anyway, so it isn't too difficult, but if we can get them to *think* they are watchful, when in fact they are not, we will have more success. In some ways, this kind of attack is preferable than an outright temptation to some great sin, for it is much more subtle, much more easy to disguise and far less recognizable to your patients. They will have a harder time changing once you have them fully ensnared because they are seldom cognizant of the need for change.

Laziness and indolence are more natural to humans than diligence and exertion. We need to capitalize on this fact. We can encourage a drowsy kind of life without them *literally* sleeping through it, though that is not such a bad idea. What I suggest is more of an overall approach to life that is characterized by taking it easy, choosing the path of least resistance, declining difficult tasks and considering all choices in light of personal convenience and comfort. The drowsy life is quite a self-centered one as serving others is not usually conducive to lethargy. These patients claim (to themselves) that they would be more than happy to help others if it "worked out" for them. Alas, it rarely does. And when one goes through life only half-awake, one is likely to miss seeing the needs of those around them. That is one of our specialties—helping our patients block those subtle promptings to do good that come from the Enemy. Drowsiness smothers the gentle nudging, for even though the voice—as described by the Enemy—is still and small, it is heard and felt only by the alert and sensitive. Service requires energy and willingness—just those characteristics that are quite opposite to the drowsy life.

The drowsy life not only precludes service but it also avoids mental and spiritual exertion. Here again, these patients go through their desultory days only half aware. There is a kind of mental and spiritual torpor that informs all action but it is comfortable enough to keep them unaware of the dangers they face. They cannot see things as they really are (see The Dull Edge of the Blade for more ideas on this), for the smoldering lamp is one that gives very little light. The oil is nearly gone, the wick is sputtering in the last few drops, and the tiny little flame is almost out. Many humans—even sometimes ardent believers—keep their lamp perpetually in this state and they become so conditioned to living in dim light they don't know any other state.

What is more important, they completely disregard their lack of additional oil. Indeed, the Enemy's parable was intended for believers. They are, ostensibly, the ones who are waiting for his coming and they must have a lamp and light when he comes. But happily, we have encouraged complacency about their "waiting" and "watching" that leaves them content with smoldering lamps. The lesson in the parable was about the obtaining of the oil, and many of your patients will have missed the point. As long as they have the lamp, they are unconcerned about the brightness of its light or the requirement for more oil.

Take the study of the Enemy's word for example. And do not, at your peril, underestimate its significance—it is his way of leading his children *to him* and *keeping* them there. You will of course have noticed that a great number of believers no longer even bother with it. The skepticism about the miracles, the archaic language, the little understood historical context—it is all too far removed from their contemporary life to be valued. That is the best state of things. For the rest, a straightforward, simple reading is sufficient. These individuals have a sincere desire to attend to that part of their religious life, so go ahead and let them read. The frequency is something we try to attack. I would suggest once a week to them as good number, especially if it is on Sunday. But the depth of the study is a more important aspect to focus on. We have come to understand that the Enemy's word is not at all effectual unless it is allowed to sink down deep inside them. Unless they actually dig through to a depth where they can extract some nuggets of his gold ("Fool's Gold" of course...) *and* unless they take what they have discovered and allow it to change their daily life, it will not have been useful. However, because we have found that *can* actually happen, i.e., his word causing a change; and our efforts go toward keeping the patient's focus on the surface of the Enemy's word, avoiding the deep digging and searching. *That* is the drowsy life and the smoldering lamp-getting the barest minimum out of a mere perusal of the word.

So for those patients who really *are* trying to read the Enemy's words, encourage them to hurry through it. Turn it into a perfunctory exercise. Whisper to them, "Just read and get it over with." Notice I say *read*—not *study*—keep it to mere reading. Or even better, suggest they just listen to an audio version while they drive. They can then check it off the "to do" list without the meaning penetrating head or heart. No slow, close reading, no questioning, no pondering, no looking at cross references, no seeking of patterns, lists and symbols, no observing certain nuances of words, no contextualizing, no searching for deep meaning, and of course, no standing back (*"far reading"* I call it) to see the big picture either. In short, have them avoid all of those practices and habits that are fruitful for the *real* disciple. Don't let them get past "the itch." You know what I mean, that moment after they have sat down to begin reading and they feel this pull to get back up and get a drink, or take an Excedrin, or turn down the air-conditioner, or find their phone, or check on the sleeping infant—*anything* that gets them out of the chair is "the itch." You want to interrupt the moment, for if they ignore "the itch" and make it past that point, there is a very real possibility they will have some meaningful study.

Another thing that is helpful here is to turn their attention to the many commentaries of the scriptures that are available. Because the Enemy's words are often difficult to comprehend, especially those that have been translated frequently (think Isaiah here), it is slow going and takes more effort than most humans want to expend. If you push them off onto the published commentary rather than the actual scriptures, they feel good about themselves and never realize that they are getting the word second-hand or diluted, or farther from the actual source. You see the commentators have paid the price to understand. *They* have made the Enemy's words their own and while other readers can certainly derive some benefit, commentaries cannot take the place of the actual words themselves. Remember the plea of the foolish virgins for some oil? It simply *cannot* be given to another, but must be obtained for oneself.

What we work against is the Enemy's ultimate desire for everyone to "speak in the name of God," because they know his word and thereby his will. They come to know *him*! The reading of the commentary will make the patient feel like he has studied without encountering the Enemy's words first-hand.

Once again, a drowsy sort of study resulting in a smoldering lamp, for the real oil found in serious study of the scriptures has not been acquired. And fortunately for us, the oil they may have gathered from serious study in the past, *will not last*! That is, of course, a slightly different avenue of attack. A number of patients will have had some serious study in the course of their days, but for whatever reasons, have slackened their efforts. Keep them making the assumption that they are still "good to go," as the quaint colloquial expression says. Remind them of those past days that they have profited from and persuade them in the belief that, unlike eating and drinking and sleeping, they have had the benefit and can keep going for some time on that small amount of "oil" they purchased years ago. Thus, the lamp will be smoldering and they won't notice. Thankfully for us, it will eventually go out altogether.

Best,
Wormwood

Install the Misting System

My Dear Tempters,

You need to spend more time thinking about the nature of your work as a tempter. One of our basic tenants down here is based on the premise that humans will inevitably stumble and fall during their mortal existence. If we can *cause* the stumbling, so much the better, but if not, we *must absolutely* exploit each and every stumble for our own ends.

First, I will discuss our efforts as causal agents. What we hope to accomplish with each human who walks on the path back to the Enemy is to create disruption, confusion, and distraction. I have already suggested numerous ways in which we can achieve this in previous e-mails. Our most effective weapons are like a very fine mist of darkness, which, at first, is hardly even felt and only vaguely recognized as obscuring sight. Eventually, we can increase the density and spread of the mist until it is almost like walking in darkness during the daytime. This cannot be achieved all at once, so do not be in such a hurry. It must be gradual to prevent a defensive response on their part. The advantage of the darkness coming in a mist is that they keep going instead of stopping. They get used to a daily walk in dim light. As the darkness deepens, a stumble and fall is more likely, but it is also the perfect time to give a slight nudge until they are *no longer on* the path. They are usually cognizant of an actual fall, but a gradual alteration of direction is less discernible. The darkness produced by the mist is what helps change the course.

Now we can cause this darkness, but we cannot always cause humans to abandon the path because of it. You see, even though we are spreading the mist over *everyone* (just observe what drastic cultural and societal changes have taken place lately), humans have the uncanny ability to keep unwaveringly to the path. We cannot quite determine exactly how they are able to continue walking straight when we have covered the entire earth with such a dense, dark fog! But some few of them are not hindered on the journey because *something* keeps them from the aforementioned disruption and distraction.

They appear to have some kind of internal light available that we have not yet been able to identify. That is why we must energize our efforts to produce a darkness that completely obscures the light. Blindness is what we are working for here. Complete blindness is the ideal, but we will also accept varying degrees of blindness as that will facilitate the detours we put in their way. This blindness I speak of is the inability to see things as they really are and, of course, the inability to see the Enemy. A perfect example of our efforts to deepen a dark mist is pornography. In ages past, we were certainly producing the stuff, but getting the product to the humans was more difficult due to society's standards—a mist of darkness but a fine one, if you will. However, in recent years we have successfully made the mist of pornography darker and denser than ever before and now, thanks to the loosening of moral standards it is easily obtained, potent in its effect and almost impossible to overcome. For so many, the darkness is now impenetrable. It makes partakers blind—helplessly and completely blind—and it causes destruction in its wake.

In this endeavor, we work alongside those humans we have already made loyal to our Father. They can be a great help to you. Get your patients to listen to these "alternate" voices. We have trained them to mock the very path itself and those on the path. Use their influence to cause your patients to feel embarrassed by even *being* there—use social media here. Mockery and light-mindedness are quite effectual. We have conditioned these helpers to focus on youth, beauty, clothes, entertainment, sophistication, pseudo-intellectualism, and any kind of excess. They pride themselves on being atheists who are too intelligent to be fooled into believing in the Enemy and his pathetic followers. Organized religion is anathema to them. Our human advocates can be extremely effective in persuading your patients to willingly leave the path in pursuit of Babylonian things. They have come to love the darkness that we spread. It gives them cover, you see, for all they desire to hide from the light. They fear the light and are only too happy to stay in the dark. And their misery loves company.

Now secondly, I want to mention our work in taking advantage of the stumbling and falling that is merely the "reality of mortality" as one follower described it. As mentioned in an earlier e-mail about adversity, the Enemy knows that his children will fall. He is interested in their getting up and becoming stronger. He knows they will stumble on the path he has set for them. He knows they may occasionally step *off* the path—it is quite narrow after all. But he also knows they can *always* get back up and back on. He provides both the choices and the helps to do just that. I will not repeat here the terrible slander on our leader about this subject, so don't expect me to.

Our job is to get into the thick of it just after the trip and the fall and prevent the getting back up. Whether we ourselves have caused the fall or whether it is a result of their mortal experience matters not. We can capitalize on both. Here the blindness and darkness helps. One approach is to administer a large dose of self-reproach. A slight whisper filled with demeaning derogatory slurs, you know what I mean—the kind they would *never* call anyone else—they are very willing to label themselves. Stupid, moron, loser, idiot, failure, the list is endless! This kind of self-name-calling is not at all repressed by the "love thy neighbor" injunction or the "as I have loved you" axiom.

For some reason, they think the worth of a soul does not apply to self. So, with our help, they beat and batter themselves to the point of spiritual and emotional exhaustion, and then the effort of getting back up and moving forward is simply too much. Strangely enough, this works whether they have succumbed to our initial temptation to sin or whether the circumstances in life have brought them low. The mists of darkness will foster criticism of self—for because of their inability to see things as they really are, they are convinced that everyone else is flourishing along the path. Comparisons with others are nice, hot fiery arrows you can shoot here.

Discouragement after a stumble is a viable avenue of attack. If the fall has been particularly painful, preventing the patient from getting "back on track" is likely going to be easier. Here our whisperings take the form of reminding how painful it was to fall and how hard it will be to get back up. Encourage the false assumption and expectation of "catching up" to others. This view of the "race" of life is good because, once again, we employ comparison. When humans compare themselves to one another, discouragement follows discouragement. Remember that women's race in the Olympics that one year when the barefoot runner got in the way of the favored runner and she tripped and fell? Rather than get back up and start again or at least admit it was unfortunate but she could try again next time, we made sure of the outcome. Shlublus, who was assigned to her, jumped right in with urgent whispers, and she was carried off the track crying and soon in front of the press blaming the barefoot runner for the whole thing. Blaming others for missteps and stumbles is very helpful to our cause; it might even be preferable to them blaming themselves as it typically precludes any change. In other words, it prevents humans from getting back up and on their way or at least postpones it so we can move them more firmly into the darkness. So what we hope for is—figuratively speaking—the trip, the stumble, the fall, the crying, and the blaming and, thus, no moving forward on the path to the Enemy.

Now, a word of caution about this path-walking business: the Enemy's most ardent followers have developed an uncanny ability to reach out and pull back on to that very narrow path, those patients we have influenced to stray. Even more nefarious is a human-chain kind of response for those who are *way* off the path—patients who we may have had securely in our camp, who happily joined the mockers, who long ago lost their sight, who have been wandering aimlessly for years in our own broad avenue—*they are at risk!* For holding on to one another's hands and involving many in the effort, the reach of this rescuing strength and security can be extensive. Don't let them anywhere near your patient! And do not assume that your patient is *ever* far enough away from the path that he cannot be retrieved by the Enemy. We have unfortunately found that there is *nowhere* this powerful chain of believers cannot reach. Keep them as firmly in the company of the scoffers and the entertainers as you can. Remember, *we* do not believe in the blind recovering their sight. Keep the darkness misters on continually!

Best,
Wormwood

The Fear Factor

My Dear Tempters,

I hardly know where to begin with this subject as it pervades almost all of our efforts. What I want to discuss in this e-mail is *fear*. It is not as difficult as it might seem to spread this type of fertilizer on the lawn of our destruction. Fear is a vital ingredient for the kind of growth we want.

Below is a brief list of some of the various aspects of fear we incorporate in Our Father's work.

1. *Fear of the Enemy and his judgment.* This has declined in recent years with the upswing in the total rejection of the divine, but it is still effective. With this approach, we gather all the "hell fire and brimstone" verses of scripture and create within our patients the image of a vengeful, angry God that will cause fear and trembling and turning away—not only in the day of judgment, but even here and now. Dismiss the gentle healing picture of the Enemy and focus your patients instead on the Michelangelo type figure of condemnation (i.e., The Last Judgment, Sistine Chapel). The outstretched arm of invitation that Isaiah was so fond of mentioning is instead brought down in disapproving wrath—at least it will be if we have it our way. It shouldn't be hard to generate this fear—the texts describe the day as dreadful, after all!

2. *Fear of failure.* This is a most fertile field. Human tendencies (especially as they become adults) lean toward the negative and the hesitation to act because of the fear of failing is common. This is absolutely *vital* when said act is an inclination toward change for the

good. Jump immediately in to the conversation they will have with themselves. Add your suggestions about the level of difficulty. Advise taking more time to think about it. Warn them of the uncomfortable and possibly painful days ahead. Remind them of past failures. This is especially effective when trying to overcome bad habits. Surround them with fellow "fear mongers" who will chime in with their own stories of failure. All of these techniques will work, whether the endeavor is improving one's language or repenting of adultery. The ultimate aim, of course, is to halt the change. Use fear!

3. *Fear of the World.* We generate all sorts of fears that are unrealistic. We are able to do so because the fears are based in real life but are stretched by the imagination, so far from rational thought, the fear becomes a phobia. We start with the daily news and build into a crescendo of alarm and dread that ultimately produces an almost catatonic state of being. With this approach, you pull up all the gruesome mental imagery about actual world conditions: disease, terrorists, petty criminals, drug cartels, flu epidemics, stalkers, thieves, bullies, drunk drivers, cyber-attacks, hacking, overpopulation of the world, communism, economic depression, etc. Draw from the whole range of social problems that are readily available. If those are not effective, you can move on to earthquakes, mudslides, tsunamis, hurricanes, tornados, global warming, drought—you have the whole gamut of Mother Nature to work with. Next, you might have your patient read as much as possible about a particular fear in order to increase his anxiety by more detailed information. Keep the imagined scenarios playing constantly in his mind. They will soon have enough trepidation about possible calamities—they will hardly leave their bed, let alone their home. The subsequent isolation will leave them vulnerable for even greater attacks.

4. *Fear of sharing their belief in the Enemy.* Especially in today's cultural climate, it is a fearful thing to talk openly and positively about (what we have caused to be) "old-fashioned" morality and religion. We have persuaded humans that they infringe, they offend, they cause discomfort, they "step on toes," they "push religion down

throats"—if they open their mouths and follow the Enemy's injunction to "preach the gospel to all the world." So your job is to whisper these disquieting phrases just as they are about to speak. Pump in the fear: fear of feeling stupid, fear of not knowing the answers to hard questions, fear of being ridiculed, laughed, at or simply ignored.

There are myriads of other ways that fear can be worked into our great offensive. With persistence and the deepening darkness of the world, it should be easy enough. Just be sure to keep them away from the Enemy as much as possible so they will not recognize your manipulations and distractions. The closer they are to the Enemy, the more easily our strategies are discerned and dismissed.

Best,
Wormwood

HUNTING THE YOUNG

My Dear Tempters,

One subject not specifically addressed in these e-mails is your attention to the younger species of humanity. In the past, we focused directly on the older generation because that was where we were most effectual. However, we have now entered an entirely new phase of diabolicalness, and I can assure you that any effort you make on the youth will be rewarded tenfold—by the time they are sixteen, they will be ours! There are several angles from which to aim your weapons.

I will briefly list a few of them here:

1. *Create a consumer market of children and adolescents.* A hundred years ago, adults were the only consumers of products. Children and older youths did not generally have an income, and parents supplied their needs (notice the word). Now, in response to our work, young people are target groups for advertisers and manufacturers. It is the youth to which they direct their schemes and ploys—from positioning the products at their eye level in stores, to the blaring commercials that inundate the airwaves. We have trained young people to consume, to want, to beg, to plead, to whine and whimper, and finally to *get!* So spend time on this area. Put the young in the way of products and promotions and fix the addiction firmly in place, at least by the age of eight.

Parents will be your unwitting allies here as they get so tired they are inclined to give in to the pressure if it will buy them a moment's peace. They cave in quite easily and will eventually accept the ever-growing obsession with "things" their children have acquired and assume it is just how life is. Turn the wants of the children into their needs. Don't let the mother get out of the store without buying them *something*. It will make it more difficult each time. Then as your youth get older, they will seek employment for the simple reason that they want to *buy*. This has the happy effect of moving their attention away from education to shopping. Always keep them aware of the latest product, as well as what their friends have.

2. *Create a need for constant entertainment.* Once again, this was in the past a weapon for adults because children found ways to entertain themselves. They read stories, they explored outdoors, made forts, played spontaneous games, ran around just for the sheer joy of it, and most of all, used their imagination! That is where we have been so successful in recent years, and technology is the key. Children used to be adept at creative play, both by themselves and with others. They could fashion any device or structure or plaything out of what was at hand. They went to the moon, explored caves, and fought battles— all through imagination.

Now they need expensive toys that usually break shortly after purchase and which they lose interest in quite soon. They find they cannot possibly play Star Wars without a light saber—preferably one that makes the requisite annoying sound. If you work diligently on them, you can get your children to have such a dependence on being entertained by some*one* or some*thing* that they are a complete mess before the age of five. You do this mainly by giving them a "screen." Now that we have saturated the adult world with our screens, we have moved on to hook the younger generation. We have found it very fruitful. It can begin with Sesame Street, Dora the Explorer, Paw Patrol, and a Disney movie now and then; but it will soon develop into a constant desire to have a phone or tablet in front of them. Because one can now pull up a movie or game instantly—thanks to the Internet—there is an unending variety and constant availability of screen temptation. The aforementioned tired parent will begin with an occasional hand off of the phone—just for a minute. But the joy they find in the cessation of whining will generate a continual succession of "just for a minute" times.

We have parents who willingly hand over a four-hundred-dollar cell phone to a three-year-old with sticky fingers! It even amazes us! So your work here begins with the parents but then, as the child grows older, keep his focus on the screen, increase the time, downplay any fun that happened apart from a screen and move his focus to other movies, additional games, and longer time periods spent dumbly watching. The more they watch, the less inclined they are for other activities. More importantly, if you start young and use children's entertainment first, it will not be difficult to advance to your next level. A smartphone in the hand of an adolescent is a direct path to pornography, and it is now *their phone*—hence, available at all times!

3. *Lose the language.* Screen time has a secondary effect—it retards the development of language. More and more children are learning language at a slower pace and a later age, and much of the change is due to the time they spend in front of a screen. When humans sit dumbly in front of the screen, words are heard but not read or expressed; hence, they do not become part of their vocabulary. Work hard at preventing the acquisition of words and then as they get older, try to shrink the number of words to a very small number—that will help limit communication. Bring in the contemporary, colloquial jargon that is as banal as it is imprecise. We love the deterioration of language—it is one of our happy accomplishments.

We have been hard at work even since Johnson's 1755 dictionary. Your patients do not realize the deleterious effect the loss of language has on them, and if we can help it along at an even younger age, what a triumph! The shrinking of vocabulary affects the ability to communicate successfully, and this in turn has a decided impact on relationships. For relationships are dependent on communication, and when that is corroded, so is the relationship. Try to get your youth to stop talking to one another face to face. That will create an aversion to *real* communication. Sure, they can send a short text, but it is just not the same. They will soon be adverse to looking into another's eyes and completely unable to read facial expressions, or listen patiently.

4. *Make them grow up too soon.* This really begins with the parents, and is closely connected to numbers 1 and 2 above. Simply put, this is where you rob children of their childhood. You have a couple of options here, You can get them into sports very early and create the illusion in their parent's minds that they are a good candidate for the Pros or the Olympics, thereby forcing them to spend six hours a day practicing. This will leave no time for just being a typical child or behaving like a normal teenager. The obsession justifies the inordinate amount of time in one single endeavor. There will be an occasional pro athlete or Olympian, but for most, it will just end up as a costly but very narrow adolescence. In the meantime, their life is out of balance.

Another approach is to get them attached to worldly images and viewpoints very early in life. You can achieve this with young girls by having their parents push the "pageant" life. You know what I mean—you have seen the photos—little girls of five with their hair all sprayed and glittered and their eyes made up, mincing around in skimpy little outfits. It would never occur to them to wear such things or move their bodies in such suggestive ways were it not for mothers who promote it. So before they are ten, the way their body looks, the way their hair is cut and what they are wearing become far more prominent in their minds than they should be at that age. Five-year-olds have always played dress up but it was never based on the "sexy, skinny woman" image until recent years. This approach is related to the Silly Women Syndrome as we strive to get young adolescent girls to view themselves like a Victoria's Secret model. The earlier we can get girls and boys (use pornography there) to focus on their sexuality, the easier time we will have with our entrapments as they get older.

Push the parents, especially the mothers, to constantly take photos of their children and post them on social media. What begins as an innocent thing will have a long-term effect on the children as they grow up, especially young girls. They will be so intently focused on themselves and how they look, documenting every day of their lives; they can be so easily distracted from more important things the Enemy has in mind for them.

5. *Make the "dark" attractive.* This is a rather new weapon we have formed. Humans feel both a fascination and an aversion—in equal parts—to many things they ought to outright reject or avoid. You've seen them when they pass by a bad car accident: the slowing of the traffic comes not from avoiding the emergency vehicles but from the craning of necks as they look with a morbid fascination for the bloodied body lying on the stretcher. They experience both dread but also desire. From the days of Roman Colosseum spectacles, humans have always been part of our "spectator sport." Even if they abhor something, they want to see it. They feel that attraction/aversion about mental and emotional illness, interested spectators. Well now, with these adolescents, we have moved them from spectators to participants. If they do not have some emotional or mental malady, or at the very least, a healthy dose of teenage angst, we help them *think* they do—precisely because, through movies and books, we have made it look darkly appealing. Our goal is to have them become not just merely inured to pain and darkness around them, but almost desperate to procure it for themselves!

Remember the now-banned cigarette advertisements? We never used an old, lined face or a gravelly-voice cougher to sell the product. No! We used only the most beautiful women and healthy, masculine men to promote a product that produced neither beauty nor health. We now do the same thing with depression, mental illness, and melancholy. We find a young, pretty, wide-eyed, innocent looking actress and give her some appealing dialogue and mournful expressions and we soon have teenagers wishing they were depressed or telling themselves they are. Remember *Girl Interrupted?* Instead of forgetting themselves and playing kick-the-can in the neighborhood, they will gravitate back to the screen (see #2 above) and imagine all sorts of problems. The kick-the-can days are over—I am happy to report—because thanks to us, even the most dreadful (in human opinion) of events, such as suicide, can be made attractive if we are sedulous enough in our efforts. Hollywood is your best friend here.

6. *Bad examples.* This is especially effective when the examples they follow are their own parents. Here, your work entails getting children to be within hearing distance when their parents complain, criticize, condemn, denounce, and pass judgment. This is especially effective when such pronouncements are founded on ignorance and bigotry. You can effectively turn a six-year-old into a racist by having them absorb their parents vitriol and corrosive diatribes. If you cannot get the parents to set a bad example, try to get your patient to spend time at his friend's house in the hope that they may hear it there. Children are very easily influenced and a father's patronizing chauvinism toward females is *so* very easily passed on to the next generation.

Focus your efforts on these five areas and you will be following one of our most cherished dictums—get them while they are young—for a tender fledgling is much more vulnerable than a strong mature bird in flight.

Best,
Wormwood

My Dear Tempters,

Please keep in mind our Manifesto which affirms our intentions concerning every one of the Enemy's sons and daughters. Our declaration of rebellion was given long ago in that vast realm of the fallen and has remained our stated platform ever since. I have included it here in this e-mail for your review:

The Manifesto of Malevolence

Due to the injustice of the Enemy and the everlasting enmity of Our Father, as heaven's fugitives, we proclaim our unremitting crusade to fight against light and joy and all things good and righteous. Armed with hell-flames and fury we wage by force or guile, eternal war. *

With the overarching and undergirding focus on the destruction of the family, we will position our soldiers and deploy our forces with as much dark power as we can amass. We resolve to completely surround them, continually seeking to form novel weapons of war and new combinations of wickedness.

Our work commences on lies and continues through falsehood. We use a truth to promote a lie, we shall alter, subvert and transform to mislead. We seek to deceive and blind.

Darkness is our constant companion.

---

* Milton, *Paradise Lost*, 1.21, II.61

We vow to distract and distance the human race from the Enemy above and drive all before us to Our Father below by the exploitation of man's fallen state.

We vow to create division and disrupt unity. We promise to isolate and separate, generate differences and divide men and women, families and friends, nations and peoples.

We promote misery and enslavement, chains and bondage, suffering and servitude, unhappiness and dread. Agency will be forever thwarted.

And all this, if not victory, is yet revenge.[*]

Now go forward, commit this to memory, abide by its precepts and do your work!

Best,
Wormwood

---

[*] Ibid., 11.104

ABOUT THE AUTHOR

A dele H. Lewis is an Arizona native. She is an instructor in Art History at Arizona State University. She and her husband Ken have six children and twelve grandchildren.

CPSIA information can be obtained
at www.ICGtesting.com
Printed in the USA
FSHW012155030219
55457FS